Winifred Fortescue was born in a Suffolk rectory on 7th February, 1888, the third child of a country rector and connected, on her mother's side, to the Fighting Battyes of India.

When she was seventeen – in order to ease the strain on family finances – she decided to try to earn her own living and went on the stage, performing in Sir Herbert Tree's company, and later starring in Jerome K. Jerome's *The Passing of the Third Floor Back*.

In 1914 she married John Fortescue, the King's Librarian and Archivist and famous historian of the British Army. The marriage, in spite of a huge disparity of age between them, was a uniquely happy one, and although Winifred Fortescue gave up her career on the stage, she later began a successful interior decorating and dress designing business until illness forced her to close her company down. It was at that point that she began writing, for *Punch*, the *Daily Chronicle*, the *Evening News*, finally inaugurating and editing a Woman's Page for the *Morning Post*.

In the early 1930s, John and Winifred Fortescue, now Sir John and Lady Fortescue, moved to Provence and there she wrote her famous and bestselling *Perfume From Provence*, and the sequel *Sunset House*. *Perfume From Provence* became a bestseller once again when it was re-published by Black Swan in 1992. *Trampled Lilies* continues her story of Provence during World War Two. Her autobiography, *There's Rosemary, There's Rue*, was first published in 1939. She died in Opio, Provence, in April 1951.

Also by Lady Fortescue

PERFUME FROM PROVENCE
SUNSET HOUSE
THERE'S ROSEMARY, THERE'S RUE

and published by Black Swan

Trampled Lilies

BY
The Honourable
Lady Fortescue

BLACK SWAN

TRAMPLED LILIES
A BLACK SWAN BOOK: 0 552 99706 4

Originally published in Great Britain by
William Blackwood & Sons Ltd

PRINTING HISTORY
Blackwood edition published 1941
Black Swan edition published 1997

Black Swan Books are published by
Transworld Publishers Ltd,
61–63 Uxbridge Road, London W5 5SA.
in Australia by Transworld Publishers (Australia) Pty Ltd,
15–25 Helles Avenue, Moorebank, NSW 2170
and in New Zealand by Transworld Publishers (NZ) Ltd,
3 William Pickering Drive, Albany, Auckland.

Reproduced, printed and bound in Great Britain by
Cox & Wyman Ltd, Reading, Berks.

TO

THE SOLDIERS OF FRANCE

*FOR WHOM, AND WITH WHOM, MADEMOISELLE
AND I WERE SO PROUD TO WORK*

*WITH SORROWFUL PRIDE, BUT WITH A GREAT
HOPE, I DEDICATE THIS BOOK.*

WINIFRED FORTESCUE.

SUSSEX, 1941.

CONTENTS.

CONTENTS

Trampled Lilies

CHAPTER I.

GENERAL MOBILISATION

THOUSANDS upon thousands of French soldiers, unshorn, sweat-begrimed, exhausted, marching, always marching in a kind of despairing sleepy stupor; some falling out of rank and dropping down upon a roadside bank to unlace heavy army boots—filled with blood. One man, stumbling along with a curious white bundle in his arms, his motherless baby. We found out afterwards that he lived in a lonely place, his wife had died only a few days before he was called up. There was no one left to take care of the baby; no time to find a foster-mother for it and no money to pay her if she could have been found. And so he joined his regiment with his baby and marched away with it in his arms until some compassionate women rescued it and will tend it for him until he comes back.

Will he come back?

The peasants of our village lined the roads for hours to watch this endless sad procession. Their husbands, fathers, sons, and brothers had all been called up two days before. Were *they* looking like these men now? Were *their* feet bleeding ? Such were the anguished questions one read in those women's eyes as they clutched their children closer to their sides. Suddenly a rough-looking *poilu* of middle-age broke rank and, striding up to one of our young mothers who was holding up her baby boy to see the soldiers pass, gruffly asked her if he might kiss the child. All the women began, hopelessly, to cry.

Up and down and in between those dusty ranks of men ran lost and limping dogs, hunting and sniffing tirelessly along the lines in search of masters who had, perforce, left them at home. They had broken loose and followed—better this dusty dangerous life of the open road, sustained by the hope that in another moment the familiar scent of the beloved master would reward that faithful questing nose ; better the evils of possible hunger and thirst, the incessant risk of being crushed by passing cars, than lonely captivity without him, listening eternally for the one step, the opening of a door in that particular way——

Happily, all soldiers love dogs, and these persistent searchers are adopted—and over-fed—the officers turning a blind eye in the direction of these pathetic camp - followers. Indeed, one officer told us that to keep *poilus* happy and content one dog per ten men would be necessary. We rescued two of these wanderers, but never succeeded in comforting them. They just waited patiently until a door was inadvertently left open and then they stole out swiftly to resume their search, and we saw them no more.

This is *Mobilisation Générale.* How few of us, even we English and Americans living in France, had realised, even partially, the full meaning of those two words ; how they could paralyse every vital industry of the nation in one day ; how they could kill the happiness and tranquillity of every home. Well, we soon learned their dreadful significance ; for suddenly we English, living in a little lost village perched on a peak of the Alpes Maritimes, became a great military centre. We are well placed strategically ; we are well hidden amid olive-groves. *L'État Major* was established on our mountain. We were living in *Le Quartier Général* and under Military Law.

Our personal share in the national agony began with the visit of a be-starred General who, with his staff, visited all our houses in turn asking us, with a beautiful courtesy, if we could, perhaps, house some of his officers and his men. A year before, when war first menaced, we had put our houses, our gardens, our cars—and ourselves—at the service of the French Army, so that this visit and this request found us long prepared with lists of all the accommodation we could joyfully offer. Our one fear, since war was declared, had been that the French Army would find no use for us. This fear was swiftly proved to have been unfounded. During the ensuing days we were to find that everything we had to offer was pitifully inadequate when hundreds of weary men stumbled into our courtyards and sagged, overladen by their heavy knapsacks, against our walls, looking at us dumbly, with pleading eyes, hoping that we would not resent their invasion; would give them shelter and, perhaps, be kind to them. We had already housed their officers in our bedrooms; on divans in our sitting-rooms and camp-beds in our corridors; every mattress, every pillow, every sheet and blanket had been unearthed from cupboards, store-rooms, and attics, their place taken by our clothes and personal posses-sions, hurled hurriedly into them when we knew that French officers were to occupy our rooms. Now we must find place for their men. Garages, stables, laundries, and out-buildings must shelter them. We scoured the country for planks to cover earth and cement floors; for straw to cover the planks. I tore my evening dresses out of their protecting linen bags which I stuffed with straw to form mattresses; the gardener ransacked the potting-shed for empty sacks and olive-sheets; for straw *paillaissons*, used for covering greenhouse frames in winter; we lent mats and rugs and carpets. Many of the men had not yet received their army blankets (imagine the gigantic task, and expense of providing for six million men from the skin outwards, not to mention arms and equipment; and, because of that sudden and ominous German-Italian pact, it had been necessary to mobilise every reservist at once).

4

Our supply of blankets being exhausted, we dragged forth bath-mats and *peignoirs* to cover the men, anything and everything that might give some warmth; rushing up and down our mountain, to and from each other's houses, in the vain hope that a neighbour might perhaps be able to lend us another camp-bed, deck-chair, or cushion; to return, breathless and discouraged, having been greeted by that neighbour with a request for something for *her* soldiers which we could not supply.

Rain began to fall. It deluged down, and our rough roads, hacked up by military traffic, became morasses. We splashed about in oilskins and high rubber boots, wanted everywhere at once, from dawn till dusk, followed by our damp and despairing dogs, who found soldiers in all their special haunts and could not be unleashed in country lanes for fear of their being crushed by army cars.

We were all leading the strangest kind of life; so strange that it seemed unreal, for all its tragic reality. To hear cars and motor-bicycles roaring ceaselessly along our lonely mountain roads, bringing officers or despatches to *L'État Major*, the newly arranged holiday home of our English neighbour, known to the peasants as *Monsieur le Marquis;* to hear typewriters tapping in Mademoiselle Pauline's laundry (now the office of a Colonel of infantry), replacing the cheerful splashing of water and the laughter and gossip shared by her gardener and washerwoman; to see a little Red Cross sign affixed to a cypress hedge leading to the Studio, now the *Infirmerie* of *Mademoiselle* of the Château below me; and the notice, COIFFEUR, nailed to the door of her secret garden with an arrow pointing towards her stable where an army barber could daily be seen cutting the hair and shaving the chins of *poilus*; to walk through the olive-groves surrounding our four houses and to see horrible zigzag trenches (immediately dug by the *Génie* in case of Italian bombardment) disfiguring terraces starred with flowers in time of peace; a *mitrailleuse* posed on the roof-terrace of my little 'Sunset House,' another beside the log-shed; and the bread and wine of the French soldiers—a fitting Sacrament as it seemed to me—on the altar of my little chapel, for even there soldiers were sleeping.

They had arrived, in rain, at night, and this was the last refuge I had to offer. One man demurred that he could not sleep in so sacred a place. I asked him if he did not believe that *La Sainte Vierge* would prefer to know her sons dry and warm, sheltering with Her. A muttered: " *C'est vrai, ça!* " and he entered in.

I had given up my own bedroom that day to their officers who would arrive later and whom I had not yet met, and so I decided to ask *Mademoiselle* to share with me the little stone *cabanon* she has built in her garden; for she, also, had given up her bedroom in like cause. The next day an amusing incident arose from this change of quarters. I had been rushing around all day and I went up to visit my Studio hoping for time to correct another batch of proofs of my latest book, ' There's Rosemary . . . There's Rue . . .' They were coming in very slowly and irregularly, with bewildering gaps and always out of order (the fault of Hitler and not of the conscientious and meticulous staff of Mr Blackwood), and they had to be corrected, hurriedly, anywhere and anyhow, for, in general, all my rooms were full of soldiers. On this occasion, my officers being out of the Studio, I had hoped to steal a quiet quarter of an hour seated on a chair before a writing-desk instead of perched, perhaps, on a store-box or a stone wall balancing my proofs on my knee.

The kind Englishwoman who had consented to replace my dear Italian *bonne* (who had fled back to Italy fearing that her country might soon be at war with France) remarked that *Madame* looked dead tired and that she would quickly brew a pot of that sovereign British restorative—tea, and send it up in the Monty-Charge (English version of *monte-charge*, in other words, the ' noiseless and automatic ' service-lift, so called because it is neither). I objected that the Monty-Charge arrived from the kitchen into my bedroom, now occupied by two officers of Artillery. Eagerly she assured me that she had seen them both go out so that she could safely send up my tea. She bustled downstairs to prepare it.

7

Just after she had gone there was a loud knock on the garden door of my Studio—Oh, my poor proofs! Outside was standing an officer of *L'État Major*, recognisable by the lovely profusion of gold braid and decorations, and behind him, at a respectful distance, an equally unmistakable English chauffeur, easily identified by pinkness, cleanliness, and insular stolidity of demeanour. The officer had been sent by the three-star General who, having heard that I and my cars were temporarily homeless, had ordered this very large and charming ambassador to turn out the usurping soldiers. Being forcefully assured that *Madame* had no intention whatever of allowing her INVITED GUESTS to be dislodged, even if a General covered with all the stars of the firmament came, in person, to command that it be done ; and that her cars were perfectly cheerful out-of-doors, covered by tarpaulins ; after renewed protests and thanks, he withdrew with a lovely bow. The English chauffeur, who during this delay had actually become red-eared and restive, then rushed up to me to say that his ancient mistress had decided to attempt a flight, by car, to England and had stopped on her way to ask me to witness her will, for she did not expect to survive the journey. He produced the document and a fountain-pen, and, as he was too hurried to enter the Studio, I pressed the will against the door and scrawled a drunken signature. While I was doing this, I became aware of the arrival

of *Mademoiselle's* old Italian gardener, Guiseppe.
He fell upon me and, gesticulating excitedly,
begged me to go down to the Château at once
as *Mademoiselle* wished to consult *Madame*
about something. I went, and half an hour
had passed before I could return, to find that
my housekeeper had been quite unaware of my
absence.

"Well, Madam, I hope that cup of tea picked
you up a bit," she said, "and is that home-
made red-currant jelly good? I thought you'd
like some with your toast."

I had to confess that I had completely forgotten all about my tea.

"Those soldiers again, I suppose," she
grumbled good-naturedly. "Well, I shall just
haul down the Monty-Charge and make you
some more."

She hauled and hauled, there was the familiar
rumble and clanking of chains, the sharp clang
of the bicycle bell, placed considerately inside
the lift-shaft by Monsieur Coocoorooloo (who
supplied the 'noiseless and automatic') to
warn the world of Monty's arrival in the dining-
room, and a few seconds later a groan and a
thud announced his descent to kitchen level.
My housekeeper opened the door of the lift and
stood for a moment transfixed, every inch of
her broad back expressing surprised indignation.

"Well, I never!" she gasped. "Your tray's
EMPTY, Madam! That blessed lootenant must
have come in, thought the tea was for him—
and cleared the lot!"

That incident refreshed me more than the tea would have done. Later in the evening, when I went down to the Château, *Mademoiselle* said to me: " I met a very smart Lieutenant coming out of your olive-grove this afternoon. He made me a beautiful bow, and thanked me for my delicate attention in sending him up such an excellent tea. He said it had done him great good. I didn't know what he was talking about and so I smiled graciously and said, ' *De rien, Monsieur, de rien.*' "

So the Lieutenant got my tea and *Mademoiselle* got his thanks. But I got a great deal of amusement.

It was the most extraordinary sensation to become an alien in one's own house and garden. I was for ever forgetting that my hall-room had become the *bureau* of a Colonel of the *Génie* who sat there most of the day conferring with his Captain (who used my little *salon* as a bed-sitting-room office) ; that I could no longer enter any of my bathrooms without danger of discovering an officer shaving ; that if I entered my front gate I must pass a sentry with a fixed bayonet and explain my errand ; that I could not fetch a flower-vase from my loggia cupboard without disturbing an army of the Colonel's secretaries who worked there ; or telephone to any of my friends for fear of delaying some important military order to be transmitted from *L'État Major*.

In the region of the kitchen it was the same. Half-naked *poilus* surrounded the great stone reservoir of water, scrubbing each other's backs joyously and revelling in the luxury of a wash. My little *lavoir* was always occupied by soldiers washing their underclothes and those of their officers, which were afterwards draped on my vines and rose bushes to dry. Under the vine pergola, by the service door, my ironing-table had been taken out of the *chambre de repassage* (in which, now, three orderlies slept) and was used for the *potpotte* of the *poilus* who lodged with me. I wandered from familiar corner to familiar corner (rendered so unfamiliar now) like some long-departed ghost revisiting what had once been its home, now occupied by others. I preferred haunting the lower regions where I might still be permitted to spoil, a little, my *famille militaire;* for I found that the *poilus* were but great children and, at that moment, lost children who needed comforting. And the smallest thing one did for them was received with such touching gratitude—a plate-ful of grapes to enliven their *déjeûner*, a packet of their loved *Caporal* cigarettes; on a cold day perhaps some hot coffee or wine; a small mirror hung up in the *lavoir* to assist the ceremony of shaving; wet coats dried in the kitchen—little obvious things which, to them, seemed to be great and unexpected. And they were all so eager to render *Madame* service. A heavy load to be carried, and at least six khaki-clad volunteers rushed to her assistance;

always they were asking if she wanted letters
posted or errands run, and when they found
out that every morning her crop of jasmin
must be picked, one and all of them clamoured
to be allowed to help, assuring her that their
officers had told them to be useful to *Madame*
in every possible way.

With the kitchen cloths tied to leather belts
to serve as aprons, they moved along the jasmin
terraces with baskets also slung around their
waists in imitation of the professional pickers
who do this in order to keep both hands free
for plucking. And, at the end, they came
to me, beaming, to ask if I would allow
them to send *two* blossoms, each, to their
wives. Hot fists were unclosed to show me
that, in each case, only two white stars had
been taken. They explained that they were
forbidden to tell their families where they
were, but that if they could enclose jasmin
flowers in their letters their wives would
know at once that their men were safe, for
the moment, in our beautiful Midi, and would
cease to worry.

One morning, coming up to ' Sunset House '
from the Château, I saw a strange and horrible
sight.

It was one of those perfect mornings of early
autumn, the distant mountains deeply blue,
the whole lovely landscape softly radiant,
glistening with sunlit dew, every late rose
and flaming zinnia a jewel in a perfect setting,
and " the little town of dreams and deep,

sweet bells" glowing golden on its olive-clad
peak. I breathed in the spiced fragrance of
ripening grapes, violet-leaves, lemon verbena,
scented geranium, the smoke of aromatic twigs
and leaves burning on a bonfire; of coffee,
floating forth from my kitchen and, predomi-
nantly, of the jasmin even now being picked
on the terraces below my rose-garden, and
I found it almost impossible to believe
myself in a world at war—until—I saw that
horror——

Crawling painfully between the white-starred
hedges of jasmin were the heads of four strange
hideous monsters. They had enormous, round,
sightless eyes, and long trunks projected from
swinish snouts. They looked like some obscene
form of insect groping blindly among my
flowers. My heart missed several beats, and
even when my startled mind had realised what
those hideous monsters were, the chill horror
that had gripped me when I first saw them,
remained. For they were four of my *poilus*
picking my jasmin IN GAS-MASKS.

Their officer had ordered that these should
be worn for an hour as an exercise—to accustom
the men to their use. Because it was the
hour for the picking of *Madame's* jasmin the
soldiers had decided that they would pick
it while wearing their masks rather than
fail her.

I had never seen men wearing gas-masks
before, and I think the sight of them, against
that background of peaceful loveliness, brought

home to me more poignantly than almost anything else could have done the horror of this war.

I grew so fond of my *poilus*. There was the stocky, tufty-headed little farmer from Tarn who grinned through every trial, and his melancholy-faced friend, who could always make his comrades laugh over his misfortunes with his officer ; for he was an orderly who had never learned to sew and was for ever losing his one needle just at the moment when his officer asked for a button to be sewn on. There was the tall, good-natured man with the squeaky, incongruous voice whose name was Auriol and who really deserved to wear one around that blond head, for he was everyone's willing slave ; there was the dark, haunted-eyed child who was continually assuring me that he and his brother *poilus* were only on manœuvres, that soon they would be over and then he could go home again to his mother. There was the pitiful man who lost his nerve when the sergeant tried to fit on his gas-mask, fought like a fiend and then took refuge in my chapel, where he sat in a corner moaning at intervals, "*La guerre ! La guerre !*" until I implored his Colonel to give him so much to do that he would have no time to think. Then there was the lanky, awkward man who, because, he said, *he* was too busy, badgered my housekeeper to iron his officer's tunic for him on a day when she was busier still and could not render him this service. I met him

wandering disconsolately in my olive-grove,
twisting in his great hands a wisp of khaki
which looked like a drowned rabbit, and when
I said : " Now confess to me that you are not
at all busy, but have never handled a flat-iron
in your life!" he wailed : " *Madame! Je
suis agriculteur!* " How should a farm labourer
know how to wash and then iron an officer's
tunic ? *Pauvre malheureux!* There was a
Parisian lawyer and a Pyrenean priest among
my Colonel's secretaries. Always we were
being surprised by curious facts about our
men. Meeting them every day and all day
we grew to know them, and gradually they
began to confide to us their troubles and
anxieties. We had noticed a general heavy
depression during the first two weeks, unusual
in volatile Frenchmen when they are together,
even under trying conditions. We had thought
that this must be due to overstrain and fatigue,
and hoped that it would wear off in time. But
as the days passed it intensified. And then
our General told us that by some mistake their
mail had gone astray and the men had had
no letters since they left their homes, so that
they all had the *cafard*. I had had no letters
from England either. I, too, had the *cafard*,
and this gave me an opening to talk with the
men. One of them had been called up on the
day his wife's *accouchement* was due. He had
had no news from home since he left. He did
not know if she were alive—or dead—whether
he were the father of a son or of a daughter.

Another had had to leave his crops unharvested
—only a daughter of sixteen in the house,
and he could give her but twenty francs to
go on with. Most of them came from country
homes in the mountains, and their thoughts
were torn between their *patrie*, their *gosses*,
and their own little bit of soil—all needing
them equally.

CHAPTER II.

OUR FIRST *FOYER DU SOLDAT*.

IT was then that their kindly General asked *Mademoiselle* whether she and her friends could devise some way of distracting those sad thoughts of his men and to help keep up their morale. He knew that she had served the French Army throughout the war of 1914-18 ; had seen the soiled Red Cross brassard on her sleeve (which called forth from an English chauffeur, an ex-Service man, the remark : " She wouldn't 'ave that *washed*, not if you were to offer 'er a million pounds "). He had also seen, with gratitude, that other Red Cross sign affixed to her cypress trees. He had visited the small *Infirmerie* which she had installed in her Studio where she tended raw feet, sore throats, cut and septic fingers, carbuncles and other minor miseries which, nad they been neglected, might have become major misfortunes and crippled his men. He knew that the few army Red Cross clearing stations in the neighbourhood were far away and not yet fully equipped. The men at the fighting Front must first be supplied with clothes, equipment, and medical stores. The waiting

army were with us now to be likewise equipped
—but this would take time. Our narrow
mountain roads were blocked for hundreds of
miles with marching troops and guns, hurrying
to the northern and southern frontiers. The
transport and supply lorries bringing necessaries
to the reservists could not yet get through.
The General saw that *Mademoiselle* realised
all this and was doing her best to meet emer-
gencies and to supply deficiencies in the meanwhile. She, if anyone, would understand the
urgent need of his men who, when darkness
fell, were obliged to wander aimlessly in muddy
mountain lanes or sit, huddled together, brooding
in garages and barns, their gloom enlivened by
a single candle.

At once *Mademoiselle* began to organise a
foyer du soldat in our village, which contains
but 300 inhabitants and does not even boast
a *café* or an inn. After much difficulty she
found one small *festa* tent still unrequisitioned
by the army. It was only intended to hold
forty men—it was not even waterproof—but
it was gay and pretty, white, striped with
scarlet, and, *faute de mieux*, it must serve.
This was erected in the middle of the village,
and every night five to six hundred soldiers
at a time crowded into it—how, we never
knew. When they had been served with hot
coffee or hot chocolate, had played a game of
cards or dominoes, perhaps written a letter
and then listened awhile to the gramophone,
they went out and were replaced by others.

There were 1800 men on our mountain at that time. From 6 P.M. till 9 P.M. did we stand and deliver hot coffee and chocolate—sixty litres of each disappeared in less than an hour. All day long soldier-volunteers ground that coffee; all day was it boiling in huge zinc *lessiveuses* until *Mademoiselle* and her staff were half poisoned by the fumes of caffeine.

But it was so well worth while. We searched for talent among the *poilus* and found two good accordion players who amused the men for hours. Soldiers of the Pyrenees sang mountain choruses—" *Les Montagnards sont là! Les Montagnards sont là!* " will ring in my ears till I die. Soldiers from Auvergne danced *La Bourrée*—even a military policeman joined in, his neatly gaitered legs surprisingly nimble for a middle-aged *père de famille*.

When the rain descended I toured the country in search of tarpaulins with which to shelter our tent, but only three small fly-sheets could I find to cover portions of it. Under these we placed the card-tables for the men. Between our makeshifts the rain poured through, and twice a night filled the empty bottles we put on the tables to catch some of the water. We stood in mud and served beaming men with hot drinks. Better this than sitting in dark garages and barns. They were now immensely cheerful and touchingly grateful.

There was a great demand for khaki or black buttons, needles and wool and thread; for every man seemed to lack buttons in important places, and had holes instead of heels in his socks. As I watched these dear clumsy sempsters reefing together their clothes with stitches like giant's teeth; saw their Sam Weller tongues and the intent expression of eyes; heard the soft (or loud, according to the depth of the wound) swearing that announced to the watcher that the needle had stabbed into flesh instead of stuff, and the stertorous breathing that told of unusual effort, I longed to have time to do that mending myself. But my life was now so hectic that all I could do to help was to buy up every button that I could find and place them in the *foyer* to be grabbed greedily by the men.

Only one tragic incident I shall ever remember in connection with our first *foyer du soldat*. On one of those wet nights I noticed a big man, one of the *Génie*, muffled in an overcoat, sitting alone on a bench which was deserted by the other soldiers because it was directly under a leak in the tent. He was continually trying to roll a sodden cigarette which he then held to the glowing charcoal in a little brazier we had placed there to warm the damp and chilly atmosphere. Naturally the cigarette would not light, but the futile attempts persisted. In the intervals of re-rolling that wet tobacco in torn wisps of humid paper, then puffing ineffectually to make that travesty of a cigarette draw, the man, with an uncertain, bewildered gesture, swept a hand across his hair, then shot a quick glance around him to see if he were observed.

Why this extraordinary behaviour? Why not choose a dry place in the tent? Why sit under a leak with water trickling on to your head? The man worried me. At length I caught his eye and gave him a smile of encouragement, since so obviously he had the *cafard*. He stared at me for a moment with vague blue eyes, and then suddenly his face lit up and he gave me an answering smile. Then the light died out and that despairing cigarette-rolling began once more; again that nervous hand stroked back the dark hair.

I could stand it no more. I came out from behind the table where I had been standing serving out coffee; crossed to that bench and seated myself in a puddle by his side. I suggested that he should change his place for a drier one, but he assured me that he was very well where he was, nodded his head, and smiled. Every question I put to him was answered in the same way: his health was splendid, he was in comfortable quarters, he was not in any way over-worked, he was among good comrades; everything was right—yet, so obviously wrong. But my last question opened that shut door. Had he had any letters from home? No, none—and then, little by little, I drew forth his story, very commonplace in these first weeks of war, but none the less pitiful. He and his two brothers had been called up before they had been able to get in the hay harvest and the potato crop. His old parents were left quite alone in the cottage up in the mountains ; they were both infirm—they could never manage to get in their crops before the snow came—there were no near neighbours in that lonely place—their mule and cart had been taken away by the army—and they depended upon their potato crop for food during the winter, since their sons would not be there to earn money or fetch supplies—and he had had no news——

That cheerless seat, that wet cigarette, those queer restless gestures were explained.

I do not remember what I said, but perhaps he sensed my sympathy and felt that he was now not alone with his sorrow and anxiety. Anyhow, he came to the *foyer* again the next night, and this time some of the *Génie* induced him to sing.

" *Chantes un peu, To-To,*" they encouraged him, and one of them whispered to me that " *cet âme perdu* " had a beautiful voice. He looked less like a lost soul that evening and he sang sentimental love ballads, such as " *Au revoir, ma Mignonette,*" in a true tenor voice, with the curious stiff gestures of the French singing soldier ; and he sang so sweetly and with such an excess of feeling that he completely silenced the other laughing, chaffing men who left off playing cards and dominoes to listen, and when he had finished pressed him to sing again—and yet again.

At the end of the evening he followed me out of the tent and walked beside me to the parting of our ways. I complimented him

upon his singing and told him that his enuncia-
tion was so good that, although English, I had
been able to understand every word of his song.
He said that he had sung for me, and that he
had taken special care to sing slowly and clearly
so that I might be able to understand. The
assurance that I had understood delighted him.
I bade him good-night and said I hoped to see
him again at the *foyer*. But the next night
and the night after that To-To was not there.
I questioned many of the men of his company,
and at last came upon the one who had induced
him to sing for us. He told me that To-To,
le pauvre malheureux, had been getting more
and more queer in his behaviour, had had a
crise in the night, become violent, rushing about
with a loaded gun in the barn where they were
sleeping, seeing phantom Bosches. He had
terrified them all and had had to be put under
restraint. Worrying about his home had turned
his brain. In the morning he was normal again,
but his officer had sent him down to a military
hospital in Cannes ' for observation.'

Somehow I felt that if I could see To-To I
might, having already gained his confidence,
be able to calm and to help him—perhaps
succeed in persuading the doctors to send him
home, where I was convinced, the worry removed,
he would regain his balance.

I visited three hospitals in succession, but
To-To had been removed from each after other
crises. At the last I was informed that my
poor To-To had been sent to a brain hospital

far away, where he must be kept in absolute quiet and seclusion while various experimental treatments would be tried. Hopeless to attempt to visit him there, and so I returned home, heavy of heart, with the little packet of dry tobacco and cigarette papers that I had brought to cheer him.

Some weeks afterwards, on returning from an absence in the Var, I met someone in the village who told me that ' my soldier ' had been seen wandering alone up the village street, lost and lonely as ever ; that he had been seen kneeling at the foot of the Calvary. No—no one had spoken to him—all fearing him to be a dangerous lunatic.

Had he escaped from the hospital ? Or had he been released ? He had never known my name, but he knew the village where I lived, and had been happier there. Was he looking for me ? Oh ! I fear he was. To-To haunts me.

Another *foyer* incident I remember. We doled out packs of cards to the men, which were to be returned to us at the end of the evening, for playing-cards are very expensive in France. The name of each man and the number on his identification disc were entered, and crossed off when he gave back the cards. At the end of one evening a pack was missing. It had been lent to a soldier of the *Génie* who was no longer in the tent. Loud exclamations of indignation from all the other men, shamed and angry that one of their number should have stolen this pack of cards from *ces dames* who had supplied this *foyer gratuit*. I said: "It was a mistake. He slipped the cards into his pocket in a moment of forgetfulness. He will bring them back. I know the men of the *Génie*, and I swear to you that at six o'clock to-morrow evening, when the *foyer* opens, that man will bring back those cards." And he did. Whether he was sought out and hounded to the *foyer* by his brother *poilus* to save the credit of the regiment, or whether, as I like to hope and think, what I said was repeated to him and, finding that someone had faith in him, he decided to justify that faith, we shall never know. But—the pack of cards was returned.

CHAPTER III.

PORTEUSE DE PAIN.

EVEN our cars were now always busy in the service of soldiers or civilians. *Mademoiselle* had offered to fetch food supplies for her officers, and medicaments for the *Postes de Secours*, and daily sallied forth in ' *Mademoiselle Peugeot*,' her ancient grey sports car. My old Fiat saloon, ' *Désirée*,' found herself decorated with a large blue D.P. (*Défense Passive*), because during the first few days of war I had asked *Monsieur L'Adjoint*, who was taking the place of our young and energetic Mayor (now a lieutenant in the *Chasseurs Alpin* at the Front), if he would nominate me as a member of the *Défense Passive* and *porteuse du pain* for the Commune ; for the baker of the village from whence our bread came had been called up and no one was left who could drive a car to fetch and deliver bread. It had occurred to me that this was simple war work that I could do. Hence my visit to *Monsieur L'Adjoint*. I found him at work in his vegetable garden, surrounded by squealing grandchildren.

He was extremely vague about the organisation of the *Défense Passive* (the French equivalent of England's A.R.P. and W.V.S.). He had not received (or had not read) the official pamphlets issued to every Mayor of every town and village in France. Perhaps, he suggested, those pamphlets had been sent to our Mayor before he joined his regiment and had been locked for safety in some secret drawer, since *Madame* said that these papers of instructions were important. If *Madame* said that our village ought to have a D.P. centre, then certainly we must have one. How did *Madame* propose to start it ? Doubtless she would tell him what should be done, and he would do all in his power to help her. He was trying to slide all the work on to me, the dear old fox.

I told him that each member should fill in a form stating his or her accomplishments so that he would know whom to call upon in case of need. He had no forms, of course, but said that he would write D.P. on a blank sheet of paper and nail it on the Mairie door, then anyone could write what he liked upon it. He was greatly comforted to know that *Mademoiselle* of the Château had already supplied gas-masks for the village and arranged for *Postes de Secours*—the first he had heard of this. That was good news. Fortunately the English were known to be energetic, and now it seemed that they would undertake all the new and boring duties and responsibilities which would otherwise have kept *Monsieur L'Adjoint* from his vines. The *Vendange* would soon be upon him, and the problem of how

27

to find enough women to pick his grapes pre-occupied him far more than precautions against improbable air-raids.

The blank sheet of paper was produced in order that I might inscribe my name upon it as the first member of our *Défense Passive* Centre, and I was given a page torn from a thumbed note-book certifying that I was now the official *porteuse du pain*, and then the ragged slip was stamped with the rubber stamp of the Mairie. Sniffing the rich odour of onion soup which stole tantalisingly from his kitchen (for *Monsieur L'Adjoint* transacts all business in his private house to avoid climbing the steep hill to the Mairie and wasting time in an office when he might be happily and profit-ably working among his vines or vegetables. Better far that the inhabitants of the village who wished to consult him should walk—or drive—three kilometres outside the village to his private house), he now heaved a great sigh of relief, thinking that at last, surely, he had satisfied *Madame* and she would leave him to sup his soup in peace.

Every morning in future I drove down early to the village to collect my great funnel-shaped bread-baskets. The first day I found a general shortage of bread, and having made the tour of five neighbouring bakeries, with difficulty I collected but five kilogs. The soldiers had been buying up the civilian supply. Only by pretending that I wanted a loaf for myself could I get a loaf from each. The little crowd of peasants awaiting my return looked very sour when they saw my meagre *récolte*.

The next day I decided to go farther afield, and, having driven sixteen kilometres, I did eventually find an ancient baker who could give me twenty kilogs, and, if I gave him a firm order, would supply me daily with from twenty to fifty kilogs. I returned to our village in triumph and this time was received with enthusiasm by the civil population. But I did not enjoy my bread-collecting ; for the old baker was rendered extremely cantankerous by his ace-of-clubs feet which hurt him. He and his ancient wife quarrelled continually, and often he pursued her all round the bakery brandishing a *pain Parisien* as weapon, she screaming abuse of him at the top of her cracked voice as she dodged behind sacks of flour to avoid the threatening loaf. They were a most unpleasant pair. Both were too old and infirm to carry the heavy baskets and sacks, so, together, we all three hauled them from the bakery to my car. Heavy work.

Their village, also, was occupied by soldiers, and it was extremely difficult to drive through narrow streets and lanes crowded with *poilus*, gun-carriages, hay-waggons, and kicking mules. My progress was leisurely. Constantly the heads of soldiers were poked through my window, and *Madame* was asked if she could supply the owners with an Aspirin tablet, a bandage for a sore heel, or some medicament. Once a soldier-priest begged me to bring him a bottle of Sacramental wine and some wafers. This meant driving to the nearest Cathedral or Brotherhood, but one could not refuse such requests from men stranded in an isolated village of the mountains.

During my bread-rounds my car was often in use as an ambulance. It had soon become known that I had had it arranged for camping ; that the backs of the arm-chairs in front could be lowered to meet the big cushion at the back, so forming beds. Two of my soldiers slept in it at night and called it *le Ritz Hotel*. One day I was stopped by a group of *poilus* who excitedly asked me if I had seen a *blessé* lying in the road. I had not, and then they asked if they might jump into my car and go in search of this wounded man. We found him lying in a crumpled heap under a hedge beside a wrecked motor-bicycle. He was a despatch rider and had skidded and broken his ankle against a rock. I lifted out my empty bread-baskets, left them in the charge of a gaping peasant, transformed *Désirée* into an ambulance, and the soldiers lifted the wounded man into the car, climbed in after him, and sat one on top of the other in a clump. Dominie, my terrified black spaniel pup, who always accompanied me on my rounds, sprawled in a floppy goggle-eyed heap on the knees of the topmost. In this manner we drove many bumpy kilometres over rutty grass tracks and stony lanes to the nearest Red Cross Centre established in a farm on a pine-clad mountain.

I drove back, picked up my bread-baskets, and turned once more in the direction of my bakery, when my car was again commandeered by the army, this time by an officer. He asked me if I would transport some of his men who had raw feet. There were ten of them, and *Désirée* is built to carry five passengers at most, but somehow we contrived to double the number, two of the men, being small, actually sitting inside the baskets.

That morning I was very late indeed with my bread delivery.

When the news came that the men billeted on our mountain were to be moved on, destination unknown, we began to receive pathetic testimonials from them, rough sheets of paper on which were chalked the English and French flags, and which bore the signatures of all. One of *Mademoiselle's* invalids in her *Infirmerie*, a *coiffeur* in private life, now threatened with lung trouble, was urgent in his desire to rise from his bed to shampoo and wave the hair of his nurse. She, being far too busy to submit to this ceremony, begged me to accept his fervent offer to arrange my hair, since, she said, nothing would quiet him until he was allowed to do something in return for the care he had received. And so, when I returned, weary and dirty from my shift in the *foyer*, I was persuaded to sit down, have my hair soaked in eau-de-Cologne, it being by then too late for it to be washed ; and, dusty as it was, it was set in beautiful waves by the light of a candle.

I shall never forget the picture of the Studio that night. A little fire crackled cosily in a corner, its flames flickering over *Mademoiselle's* pictures on the walls ; the green-painted medicine-chest ; *Mademoiselle*, herself, sitting on a three-legged stool, her small dark head bent over a spirit-lamp as she sterilised something or other ; a big man, with a queer heart and threatened bronchitis, lying peacefully in a real bed with real sheets, his head, recently tended by his *copain*, the *coiffeur*, resting on a soft pillow, watching the long fingers of his friend stroking waves into my hair ; turning at intervals dogs' eyes, which filled up slowly with tears, in the direction of his adored *Mademoiselle* from whom in so few days he must be parted.

Soon afterwards came the eve of their departure, and then many of *Mademoiselle's malades* were in tears. Our address books overflowed with names of our soldiers and all the complicated numbers of their companies, regiments, and battalions. I was given the addresses of the wives of my men and was begged to write to them telling them that their husbands were well and gay (even if they were not) when they left me.

During those last days we fêted our soldiers and we were invited to gala luncheons and dinners with the officers. On one occasion the *menu* was decorated with sketches of our houses, delightfully drawn by the regimental artist. Always the health of our King was drunk first of all.

I do not remember much about the food we ate, I only remember that towards the end of a dinner given by the officers lodged with *Mademoiselle* (when she had the queer experience of finding herself a guest in her own house) photographs of wives and small babies were surreptitiously brought forth from pocket-books and slipped along the table for me to see. My neighbour, an artillery officer, silently showed me the picture of a lovely little girl kneeling at a *prie-Dieu*, dressed in white, her little head swathed in a tulle veil and wreathed with flowers.

" Your little girl ? How lovely she is ! This was taken at the time of her *Première Communion ?* " I said. He choked and nodded his head. The smoke of his cigar had got into his throat—and into my eyes.

When we had been thanked over and over again for our hospitality and our hands had been kissed we were ' bunched ' with flowers and presented with boxes of chocolates and crystallised fruits. The General gave each of us a pass for the army zone, endorsed with a recommendation to the Military to give us special care and consideration, the paper signed by himself.

But the greatest honour we received was when, on the last night of all, after that gala dinner with the officers, a little soldier from Marseilles, nick-named *Charlot* because of his likeness to Charlie Chaplin, came to us with a message from the *chef* inviting us to coffee

in the kitchen with the officers' servants. Of
course we joyfully went and received a wonderful welcome. The table was covered with an
odd assortment of cups, saucers, wine-glasses,
and tumblers. A soldier's tin water-bottle
with a wispy weed sticking out of its spout
formed the central decoration. We quaffed
black coffee, and liqueurs which *Mademoiselle*
discovered in her store-cupboard and brought
forth in honour of the occasion ; we clinked
cups and glasses and made very merry.

Charlot promised to revisit us after the war,
in civilian's clothes with a little feather in his
hat, and the *chef* told us a lovely story about
Charlot, who, having surfeited himself with
haricot beans for supper, had then tried to
inflate a collapsible rubber mattress, had blown
a bean into the aperture, and effectually corked
it. We all laughed, but we were very near
tears—indeed the emotional *chef* often was in
tears—for this was good-bye.

They left us in the small hours of the next
morning, and *Mademoiselle* and I crept out of
her garden *cabanon* in the sad grey light which
precedes the dawn, to watch a serpent of red
fire coiling up and around our mountains—
the serried rear-lights of army cars and lorries
taking our soldiers away from us to a destination
unknown. . . .

They had gone, but others would come,
needing our care and comfort—and then,
more. . . .

CHAPTER IV.

WE JOURNEY TO THE SNOWS.

FOR many weeks during and after *La Mobilisation Générale* in France, we English residents, who had offered to house soldiers in every corner available, were taken at our word. When one Division left our district it was immediately followed by another. Hardly had we adopted one *famille militaire* as our own, learned the names and duties of officers and men and gained their confidence, when they all marched away, and hard on their heels—indeed almost treading on their heels—came others. So inconveniently quickly were they replaced that sometimes we were waving French and English flags in farewell to one contingent when we saw, with consternation, the advance guard of the next tramping towards our gates.

At last, rendered desperate by the draggled condition of my little ' Sunset House,' I actually barred my ancient door against an incoming Colonel and his staff while I, my housekeeper, and gardener, frantically tore soiled sheets from beds, re-made those beds with fair white linen, swept, scrubbed, and dusted the long-neglected rooms until the little house regained some semblance of the cleanliness and comfort it had known erstwhile. For officers' orderlies, however full of energy and goodwill, have seldom been trained to housework. Any old rag is a duster, and when no rag can be found —well, the lungs of the orderly can always act as bellows to blow away *some* of the dust.

I placed my new Colonel and his staff in comfortable cushioned chairs in my loggia, giving them iced drinks to quaff while I Martha-d with my staff indoors.

"For an hour I intend to be mistress of my house. It must be made worthy to receive you," I laughingly explained. "Please rest awhile and enjoy my lovely view. Here are drinks and cigarettes."

The Colonel kissed my grubby hand as he obediently, and I am sure gratefully, sank into a chair. His Captain and Lieutenant did likewise. I re-entered the house, bolted the door, and resumed my spuffling.

Our last *famille militaire* stayed with us for six weeks, and as we were informed that we might now expect an interval of peace, we asked our three-star General, on the eve of his departure, where he thought that we could be most useful now. The little impromptu *foyer* that we had provided for his soldiers in our village had proved such a success, and had so cheered the men, that *Mademoiselle* of the *Château* wanted to create other *foyers* wherever they were needed. The General told us that in the High Alps he had heard that the soldiers in the lonely frontier forts and isolated villages were already feeling the cold. At an altitude of 2500 metres the summer generally breaks, with violent storms, in mid-August, heralding the approach of winter. It was now the end of October and the first snow had already fallen. If we were to install *foyers* for the soldiers stationed in the High Alps we must do our work quickly before the mountain roads and plateaus became inaccessible.

" If the men are cold we must supply them with woollen clothing as well as *foyers*," mused *Mademoiselle* that evening when we were discussing our future plans. " And I shall also take up a supply of medical stores. The men at the Front are fully equipped, but the little *Postes de Secours* in the High Alps are sure to be in need of things. I should like to make each *foyer* a three-in-one affair :—

" (*a*) A room with a stove, furnished with games of all kinds, writing-paper, books and magazines, and, of course, a gramophone or wireless-set.

" (*b*) A *depôt* of warm woollen clothing, stockings, socks, mufflers, helmets, gloves, belts, pullovers, flannel vests, and shirts.

" (*c*) A supply of medical stores for the little ills and accidents of everyday life which, if neglected, may become serious."

Mademoiselle, the inarticulate, had suddenly become eloquent, and I knew then that she had dedicated herself to the French Army and could henceforth know no peace or rest but in its service.

From that moment life became a whirl of activity. Shops of neighbouring towns were ransacked for woollens of every kind. Everyone of our acquaintance was given wool and knitting-needles and ordered to knit like mad. Houses were ransacked for good French books. One collection of about 100 books was found in an empty villa. Knowing what French books can be, we asked a discreet lady to ' vet ' them for us before we gave them to the soldiers, which was lucky, for she found only five which were possible—and she is not a prude. Chemists' shops were raided for medicaments ; yards and yards of white material were bought up for bandages, and our houses resounded with the shrieks of torn linen and calico and every serious woman's skirt was whiskered with white threads which she had no time to harvest. I rushed down in my car to Cannes and bought a 40-kilo bale of *crin végétal* to stuff pillows which could afterwards be burned.

In a very few days we had amassed enough supplies to fill three cars to the roof, and then *Mademoiselle* and I set off, she leading the procession in her ' *Mademoiselle Peugeot*,' I close behind in ' *Désirée*,' my Fiat ; Jean, a faithful hired chauffeur (well used to our odd ways and even apt on occasion to do the market-ing for all our houses), following in the rear with our camp-beds, bedding, and skis lashed to the top of his car.

It was a lovely autumn morning and I enjoyed tremendously the effects of sun and shadow on the mountains; the splashes of vivid colour made by clumps of 'burning bush' clinging to grey rocks; the silver and gold of birch trees amid the dark pines; and there was a refreshing tang in the air which, at the end of a long day of steady ascent, would intensify into the exciting icy nip of snow atmosphere.

Mademoiselle speeded before me, leaving a strong scent of onions, leeks, cabbages, and cauliflowers from the huge basket of home-grown vegetables strapped upon the dicky of '*Mademoiselle Peugeot*,' which were to feed us and our dogs. The curly head of little Squibs, her sheep-dog, poked out of the window by her side, black india-rubber nose twitching ecstatically as she scented passing smells unsmelt by us, whiskers and curly fringe blowing in the breeze, so happy to have been included in the party.

Seated by my side was my little Blackness, his domed head also poked out of the window, his Cocker ears floating like banners in the wind as he kept his amber eyes firmly fixed upon the ragged silhouette of Squibs, the lady of his love, in the car ahead.

Bringing up the rear drove Jean, dark and imperturbable, his smart Fiat saloon so camouflaged by our stores and luggage that he might have been conducting some peasant household removal, or else have been mistaken

39

for some itinerant vendor of miscellaneous goods : camp-beds, skis, bales of blankets, cushions, woollen clothing, store-cases filled with medicaments, games, tins of cocoa and condensed milk, sacks of sugar, packets of writing-paper, and out of his window poked the furled flags of France and England to decorate our *foyers*.

We bowled along steadily for hours, mounting through St Vallier, then lovely little Castellane, until a sensation of emptiness within and the insistent batting of a fat paw against my side made me realise that it must be time for luncheon. *Mademoiselle* was by this time out of sight ; for she has a Voisin engine so powerful that when the sparking-plugs need attention, mechanics always amuse themselves by putting corks on them and starting the engine. The corks fly up into the firmament and disappear into space.

Nevertheless my ' *Désirée* ' can always outstrip ' *Mademoiselle Peugeot* ' on the level and we had reached a high plateau, so that I decided to speed up to within hailing distance of *Mademoiselle*. I raced ahead for two kilometres, and, turning a sharp bend, came upon her strolling slowly towards me gnawing a chicken-bone with evident enjoyment, Squibs at her heels, joyously sniffing along the side of the road.

This unusual spectacle surprised me, for *Mademoiselle* is no walker, and she must have walked far ; for there was no sign of her car on the long stretch of straight road bordering the ravine on my left.

" Hullo ! " I shouted, " that's not fair ! Have you eaten all the chicken ? And where's your car ? "

She waved the chicken-leg nonchalantly towards the ravine, then continued to gnaw contentedly.

" Go and have a look," she said between bites.

I stopped the car and questioned her : " What *do* you mean ? " I asked.

" Go and have a look over there," she advised me, and, to indicate the direction, she threw the drum-stick over the edge of the road where there was an open space between boulders and fencing.

I got out and walked to the edge of the road, and there I stopped, shocked and sickened.

A few metres below the left rim of the road, caught only by a small clump of bushes, ' *Mademoiselle Peugeot* ' hung precariously above the ravine at a drunken angle. Far, far below, two little shining parallel lines, vanishing at the same point, marked the railway, cut into a ledge of the rock above yet another ravine down which roared a mountain torrent.

I was unable to control the shaking of my lips as I turned back, horrified, towards *Mademoiselle*. My frightful imagination, which at times so tortures me, pictured horrors that might have been—for the car was quite invisible from the right-hand side of the road along which we drive in France—not a stone had been displaced and the hard, dry road showed no trace of that awful skid. Had *Mademoiselle* been trapped in her car when it slid over the edge, Jean and I would have driven tranquilly past the place believing her far ahead of us on the road. We might have gone on for hours unsuspecting an accident, only thinking that *Mademoiselle* had 'gone vague,' as she so often does, and had forgotten that it was time to eat.

Had there been no clump of bushes—the *only* clump on that rocky precipitous slope. . . . My legs refused to hold me up any more; I sank down, shivering, upon a boulder.

"Don't look like that, Pegs. Squibs and I are here, safe and sound. Something is wrong with my steering, it is irregular and loose. I wanted to have it put right before we started, but never had time. It wasn't really in the least frightening. The car slewed across the road as I turned that bend and slid gently over the edge. Luckily I wasn't going fast. I just put on the brakes and steered for that clump of bushes and we came softly to a standstill. It all happened so quickly that Squibs just thought I had done it on purpose to give her a run, and she jumped joyfully out—and you know how terribly nervous she is. I've turned off the petrol, and, if those bushes only hold, I don't think the car will be even scratched when we get her up. I'll just climb down and have a look round her."

"Oh don't, don't, DON'T," I implored her,

" you'll slip—or the car will slip suddenly and crush you. I simply couldn't bear it."

" I adore my car," replied *Mademoiselle*, " and I must see if my poor '*Mademoiselle Peugeot*' is hurt, she is a friend of so many years," and she clambered down towards it.

Round the bend came Jean with his queer load, and seeing me seated on a rock and the two dogs sniffing happily among the scrub, he drew up his car with a grin of relief that at last we had decided to call a halt and eat. I beckoned him to me, and, leaving his car, he walked across the road still smiling broadly. I just pointed over the edge and then watched his smile freeze as he saw *Mademoiselle's* car and *Mademoiselle* in the act of climbing into it.

Simultaneously we uttered yells of protest. Just that additional weight might cause the car to hurtle down into the ravine on to the railway—and then on—and down again into the river.

" I must get my bag. My passport and *laisser-passer* are in it," she cried as she dived under the hood.

I do not know what Jean looked like, for I hid my face in my hands until after what seemed an eternity I heard *Mademoiselle's* slow soft voice by my side.

" I've got them," she said triumphantly, " and now we'll have our *déjeûner* while Jean goes to get help from the next town."

She thrust a bottle of wine, a hunk of bread, and half a chicken into Jean's car, knowing

that so experienced a chauffeur could satisfy
his hunger while driving. First taking a long
pull at the wine-bottle, Jean smacked his lips
and jumped into the driving-seat ejaculating
with emphatic nods : " *Mademoiselle a eue de
la chance !* "

She certainly had had luck in her adventure,
but luck alone could not have saved her in
such a predicament. I marvelled at her nerve
and knew now the meaning of those faded ribbons
sewn to her coat in 1918 when her war service
was over.

We waited—and waited for Jean. Of course
he must have reached the town between the
hours of twelve and two when all activities in
Provence are paralysed during the sacred two
hours devoted to *déjeûner* and digestion. It
was unlikely that he would find any garage
open, but it was also certain that he would
instinctively find the favourite café of garagists
and chauffeurs and then tell a dramatic story
to persuade helpers to curtail their repast and
come to the aid of ladies in distress. But this
would take time.

Occasional cars began to pass, and not one
of them realised that anything untoward had
happened. All that they could see was two
women and two dogs in a cluster on the edge
of the ravine. I was proved right. The accident
might have remained unremarked for hours,
even for days if—but I must NOT think about
it or I could never continue that drive.

Jean appeared at last, followed by a small

remorque with a hauling-crane and two little men. It looked pitifully small for the work it had to do, and when the men, having expressed their horror and consternation at the dangerous position of the car, had offered *Mademoiselle* their congratulations on her narrow escape and began to unwind a frayed and flimsy hawser of steel which they attached first to a rickety post and then to the underpart of '*Mademoiselle Peugeot*,' I felt that now we should see the descent of both *Peugeot* and *remorque* into that awful ravine. It took all Jean's gesticulations and eloquence to persuade them to attach two hawsers, one to each side of '*Mademoiselle Peugeot*,' but even then we saw the awful spectacle of the *remorque* being slowly dragged to the edge of the abyss instead of seeing '*Mademoiselle Peugeot*' being hauled out of it. Shouts rent the air, huge rocks were hastily rolled under the wheels of the *remorque*, and it seemed we might all be stuck there for the rest of the day unless some powerful car happened to come along and its driver consented to come to our aid. But that powerful car *did* come along. There was a rumbling roar in the distance and a gigantic sausage on wheels, a Shell Petrol lorry, came lumbering into view.

I rushed into the middle of the road so that it could not pass without crushing me, and held up my clasped hands in an attitude of prayer. With a grind of brakes the monster came to a standstill in a cloud of dust, and

45

the grinning chauffeur and his companion
climbed down and approached us. Like all
Provençaux, when they had been told our
story, had exhausted their ejaculations, and
had bowed their compliments to *Mademoiselle*
for her coolness, they became whirlwinds of
help.

I will not describe those first terrible and
abortive attempts to haul up ' *Mademoiselle
Peugeot*,' or the tornado of talk between the
six helpers. I only know that at long last she
was successfully landed again on to the road,
with hardly a scratch.

How I hated the rest of that drive ! I had
hoped that *Mademoiselle* would decide that
we should stay the night in the next town,
since it was now too late for us to reach our
destination, but, perhaps wisely, she suggested
that we should go on and get as far on our
journey as we could before dark. So I followed
' *Mademoiselle Peugeot*' as before, this time
with a bumping heart, my eyes on stalks.
I was very, very thankful when at last
Mademoiselle drew in her car to the kerb before
a little touring hotel.

Dinner was a half-hearted affair. The dogs
got extra rations—our unwanted food. Both
of us had nightmare that night.

The next day passed without incident, and
I was thankful that we did not find snow until
we had nearly reached the end of our journey
—thankful, because I had been unable to pro-
cure either snow-tyres or chains in the Midi

before we started. It was only the end of October and the ski-ing season in the mountains behind Grasse and Nice would not begin for some long time. The *jasmin* was still in flower and the people of the South still clad in summer attire. So were the first *poilus* we saw, crouched by their anti-aircraft gun in the snow wearing blue cotton trousers and shirts, with noses and hands to match. Indeed, our General was right—we *were* needed.

CHAPTER V.

THE ALPINE ARMY.

Up in the High Alps the snow-plough had
cleared the main road for the use of soldiers.
We had counted on that, but even scraped
roads can be icy and dangerous, and I hate
heights, anyway, and am terrified of skids.

Arrived at the hotel where we had booked
rooms, we received a kind welcome ; and a
pile of letters awaited *Mademoiselle.* She had
prepared the ground some weeks before, using
letters of introduction given to her by our
dear three-star General, who had written to
the Governor and other French officers quartered
with their troops in the locality, telling them
of her project. The Mayor had set apart an
abandoned house in the town which we were
to use as a *depôt* for our supplies, and after
luncheon we were to be conducted thither.

I must own that my heart sank into my
Alpine boots when I saw—and felt—that house.
It had been bought by the town only to be
destroyed, and upon its site would be built
an annexe for a neighbouring college. The
war had postponed this project indefinitely,
and the poor old house had been left to moulder,

its supply of water and electricity cut off and every modern convenience torn out of it ready for the destroyers to begin their work of demolition.

It was icy, that house. The moment that we pulled open the ill-fitting back door, having battled for some time with a rusty lock, the dank cold of the interior fell upon us. We made a dreary tour of the empty rooms, seeking everywhere a stove or a fireplace. In one room there was a small grate. Perhaps in the sodden weed-invaded garden a soldier might find some dead twigs with which to make a fire; for, on the other side of the house, a band of *Chasseurs Alpins* (sent there by a grateful Colonel to make the place more habitable) were, with misguided zeal, cutting away the nice solid turf which spread down to a gate leading into the street. They were making a pathway which, inevitably, would become a morass of mud churned up by the feet of soldiers coming to get supplies.

" Oh ! Oh ! " moaned *Mademoiselle*. " *What* a pity ! That nice hard turf ! I really must try to stop them without hurting their feelings." But orders are orders in the Army, *Mademoiselle's* gentle hints were smilingly ignored, and she was informed that the men were but carrying out the Colonel's orders.

Evidently the Colonel was a townsman. However, when she pleaded for a volunteer to find us some wood, two of the men whom I had noticed enjoying surreptitious snow-

balling in a corner of the garden and who had
since joined the group of workers, laid down
picks and shovels with sighs of relief saying
that this work was very tiring. " Snowballing ? "
I asked with a sly smile. They reddened and
then grinned broadly. They had not known
that I had seen their little game.

Soon they had lighted a fire in what was to
be our office-reception-room. Of course the
chimney was damp and so was the wood.
Acrid smoke curled out into the room, which
soon was blue with it, and *Mademoiselle* and
I weeping and coughing. The dogs escaped
into the garden, and we swiftly followed them.
Joyous to have liberty of movement, they
scampered away over the snow under the
neglected fruit trees, we pursuing them, on a
tour of discovery. Perhaps we might find some
' surprises ' in the garden.

We did.

Someone—at some time—had ordered to be
dug two square pits, one on either side of the
house. Were they intended to be trenches,
for shelter in case of bombardment ? They
were from fifteen to twenty feet deep, with
precipitous sides of wet slippery clay. They
were half-full of dark water, only lightly frozen
over. The masses of earth thrown out of these
horrible pits were snow-covered, and looked
like small mountain ranges around them. On
the top of one of these ridges danced our dogs.

If they were to slip and fall in, it would be
quite impossible to get them out. Before we

could get a ladder from somewhere they would be frozen stiff in that icy water. *Mademoiselle* and I exchanged glances of horror.

" Those must be fenced round first of all," I said, shuddering.

We called the dogs from that dangerous place, and while *Mademoiselle* was excitedly informing me that many of the neglected fruit trees had, nevertheless, quinces upon them that could be made into jam for the soldiers, I, hurrying towards her, suddenly stepped into air—or was it water? Yes, it was certainly water. A sunk barrel filled with highly-scented melted snow, but so overgrown with weeds that it had escaped my attention.

An unlady-like imprecation was startled out of me.

" Another man-trap ! " I replied to *Mademoiselle's* question : " What has happened to you ? "

" I suppose these sunk barrels were put here for irrigating the garden," I suggested when we had narrowly avoided stepping into seven.

" I *hope* so," said *Mademoiselle* darkly.

" Well, what else *could* they be for ? " I persisted.

" Drains," she replied laconically.

It took some time for soldier-volunteers to make that abandoned house habitable. Stoves had to be found and fuel to put into them ; chairs were needed, but cheerful yellow garden ones of iron were eventually lent to us by the

kind Director of the hotel; shelves had to be
put up for our stores, electricity re-installed,
and, most important of all, water was once again
encouraged to flow in pipes and *cabinet*.

Our camp-beds remained permanently in their
sacks: we never slept in that house; for there
was so much to be done in it that sometimes
we despaired of being able to open a *foyer*
there under some months. Three large empty
rooms had given us the idea of making a *foyer*
there for necessitous soldiers. One room could
be turned into a recreation room. We would
put a stove into the middle of it, install a
library, get tables and chairs, and spread out
all our games : *belote* cards, *loto*, chess, draughts,
&c. A communicating room could be used
as a kitchen (it had a tap and a sink) where
hot chocolate, coffee, and *tisanes* could be
prepared for the men. The smaller room,
on the side of the recreation room (and opening
into it), would serve as a reading and writing-
room.

On our second day we were up early and
trudged through the snow to our work. Once
again we lit that sulky fire, and this time were
obliged to remain in the room while we unpacked
our stores, being slowly smoke-cured, like hams,
all day. The news of our arrival had already
been bruited in the neighbourhood, and the
next day we had official visits from the Mayor
of the town and one of his Councillors, a divine
old man with black, kindly twinkling eyes
and the most stupendous white moustache I

ever saw on man or walrus; the Military
Governor and members of his staff; a for-
midable lady, head of the local *Centre de la
Croix Rouge*, and others, all eager to sniff over
our supplies and each and all hoping to make
an early ' corner ' in them for his or her particular *œuvre*. It was a little difficult to make
the civilian sniffers realise that we had been
sent by the Army, at the request of the Army,
and that our comforts were collected for
necessitous soldiers in the High Alps. But
Mademoiselle's smile, and gentle insistence upon
this, eventually convinced them that she could
not be over-persuaded. Over and over again
she repeated that her stores were for the men
waiting for their great ordeal and that the
men at the Front were being well looked after.
At last our visitors went away—empty-handed
—but our divine walrus lingered behind to
pat us encouragingly and whisper—

" *Continuez, Mesdames, avec votre si belle
œuvre. Que Dieu vous bénisse !* " I hope God
blessed *him* for the encouragement he gave us.

I ran upstairs to what would one day (I hoped
far distant) be my bedroom. Here we had
arranged a trestle table with all our camp
cooking equipment with which we intended
to concoct luncheons for ourselves and to
prepare food for our dogs. I was to be the
temporary cook; for, hardly had our official
and civilian visitors departed, when officers
began to arrive and *Mademoiselle* must receive
them and make lists of their needs.

Oh, what long lists ! She showed them to me when I had finished agonising with cooking utensils upstairs. One Colonel told her that the most modest request he could make for his men was for two hundred pairs of socks ; and Colonels came every day, henceforth, wanting *foyers* installed for their men, and mufflers, snow-helmets, gloves, shirts, pullovers, and always socks. We realised that our three car-loads of comforts would be about as adequate for this Alpine Army as were the five loaves and two small fishes for the Jewish multitude. But then we both believed firmly that the day of miracles was not past and that although we had emptied our two purses, more money would come—from somewhere, somehow—some time soon. And, thank God, it came.

And so when eager officers appeared, followed by soldiers with expectant eyes carrying empty sacks, we confidently filled those sacks to the brim, all of us coughing and sneezing, with eyes streaming from the smoke of that infernal fire.

The smell of wood-smoke and cooking quinces will ever bring back to me our first *foyer* in the High Alps ; for those quinces had been gathered from our garden in an icy Alpine gale, and such bits of them as were not frozen thrown into a great *marmite*, where they gently stewed (and stank) for hours and even days until, from the mush and smell, many pounds of lovely red quince jelly were evolved, and the thrifty French strain in *Mademoiselle* was satisfied. The quinces had not been wasted ; and the French soldiers, who have a passion for sweet things, would love that jelly.

But the quince crisis did not come upon us until we had weathered others. To cook so large a quantity of quinces and make jelly of them required a stove, and if I tried to write of the difficulties we had before we could find one large enough to warm the house a little and then to get it installed, I could fill pages. Everyone in the town seemed to know of a stove which could be had for the asking, but when one asked, apparently our informants had always been misinformed. In the end we bought one. But a stove is useless without coal or coke. This we ordered, and every day its delivery was promised, and every night it had not come. And then two great Feast Days came upon us, All Saints' and All Souls', whereupon all commerce was paralysed, not only for two days but for a whole week. Then a great lorry strove to bring us our coal up the snow-covered alley at the back of the house, but, being too heavily laden to climb the slope and the tyres sliding in the snow, it skidded backwards down a flight of stone steps and very nearly discharged our load through the windows of the adjacent college upon the heads of the students.

All this we heard afterwards, and in the meanwhile we blithered with cold in that icy house and awaited our coal, but, while we waited for it, the work to be done in the house advanced rapidly. A Captain sent us the carpenter of his battalion, one Félix, who lived in Chantemerle, that bleak miserable village with the lovely name. Only to look at him tore the heart ; for he had the grey pinched look of poverty and the anxious, haunted look of mountain men who know that their health is undermined by hunger and that a family looks to them for bread. The spirit of the very poor, living in lonely villages in the High Alps, is often crushed by the fight with the elements, the struggle for very existence. They have but from three to four months to plant, and then to harvest their crops, chiefly potatoes and hay, before the weather breaks and the snow imprisons them, huddled with their cattle for warmth in filthy byres and hovels. But Félix was wonderful. All his life he had suffered these hardships, but he never complained, and when we asked him if he were warmly clad under his soldier's tunic that sagged upon his emaciated body, he assured us that he was ' *très bien.*' *Mademoiselle*, hearing him cough as he worked like a madman putting up shelves for our piles of woollen clothes, deliberately walked up to him and unbuttoned the neck of his tunic—

" A cotton shirt and that's all ! " she scolded, and he, looking like a guilty schoolboy caught out in some misdemeanour, muttered that he did not feel the cold very much when working. Nevertheless, his eyes positively glittered when *Mademoiselle* asked me (for I was keeper of

stock) to outfit Félix from head to heels with
woollen things from our supplies. He worked,
if possible, harder than ever after that, and in
future we always pretended that we felt rather
faint in the middle of the morning and heated
some soup which Félix shared, and as he, also,
had suffered for days from the stench of quinces,
we gave him a large pot of the jelly for *les
petits ;* for we found out that he had a large
family.

Then there was Félicien, who came in daily
to oil locks, furnish keys, and make windows
shut. I shall ever remember Félicien by his
eyes, which always spoke, though his tongue
seldom did. They pleaded with you, they
laughed with you, they asked dumb questions,
they blessed you, and I would rather have the
benediction of eyes than any spoken blessing.

It had got abroad that our *foyer* was to be
for necessitous soldiers who had no money
to spend in cafés, and that our comforts were
for those who had no families to knit for them,
or who were so poor that they hid their needs
from those at home lest their wives deprive
themselves of the necessaries of life to send
them the things they lacked. Félix was of the
latter category, Félicien of the former, and
ere long we began to find many in the same
case as lonely Félicien. The soldier-priests
and doctors helped us here. Priests hear con-
fessions and, in some cases, God could only
approve of a little merciful breach of confidence.
And doctors sound chests and so discover

inadequacies of clothing. Had it not been for them we should never have discovered the really necessitous men ; for they were so brave that they never complained and they never asked.

With joy we noticed that our lonely soldiers very soon adopted the *foyer* as ' theirs,' and, whenever they had a spare hour or two, dropped in to help with the cleaning and arranging of the rooms, the packing of parcels, or, if they were tired or cold, just to smoke a cigarette near the stove and turn over the pages of the French illustrated magazines.

But it was on the eve of the feast of All Saints' Day that we had solid proof of this. Félix, and several of the married soldiers who lived in mountain villages outside the town, told us that we should see them no more for two days as they must go to the churchyards and decorate the graves of their dead for the great Feast. Félix, with tears in his eyes, said that he had lost three babies in Chantemerle. The other men were listening and then asked us if they might spend the *fête* in ' their *foyer*,' since they were too far from their own homes " *pour garnir les petits tombeaux*," and one of them added : " *Mais nous serons chez-nous ici*." Already they considered the *foyer* as ' home.'

An officer sent us the name of a *pupille de la Nation*, an orphan without family, lonely in a frontier fort. We had been supplied with a widowed *femme de ménage* to clean the house and help us with the *foyer*. Old Fanny had lost her husband, son, and brother in the last war, and all her heart was in this work for the soldiers. It was she who scrubbed those filthy floors, who made the quince jelly, and did innumerable things to help everybody, but she was a lonely soul, and *Mademoiselle* suggested that Fanny should be the *marraine* of this orphan soldier, send him a parcel of our comforts, in her name, and, above all, write him a letter. This she proudly did, and when the boy wrote to thank his *marraine* for her parcel, he told her that though everything she sent would render him great service, her letter had been the greatest joy of all.

Every day we had soldier visitors : the splendid men of the Alpine Army ; dare-devil *Éclaireur-Skieurs* with their Mercury-winged heels ; D.A.T. men keeping vigil by day and night watching by anti-aircraft guns in snow on lonely peaks ; gunners from frontier forts ; engineers making tunnels of wood to ward off avalanches from precipitous roads otherwise blocked impassably by snow ; soldier-priests who came to beg for medicaments for little *Postes de Secours* in isolated villages—the variety was endless, but the story always the same.

Those were the early days of the war, and although the men at the Front were fully equipped in every detail, the waiting Army could not be completely supplied at once. Twice in a year before the outbreak of war, France had to mobilise her men, and the cost had been stupendous. And France built, with her gold, the Maginot Line to protect us also. (Oh! why did she not continue it along the Belgian frontier ?)

So that we felt it to be our proud privilege to aid her a little if we could ; and the gratitude of her officers, so keen for the health and morale of their men, and that of the men themselves, was very touching and made our work seem so well worth while.

We needed this encouragement to help us to bear the most depressing weather conditions later on, when a thaw set in. We seemed to be continually drying dogs caked with snow and mud ; and poor old Fanny was nearly driven to despair by the havoc made of her recently scrubbed floors by the Alpine boots of soldiers, covered with icy slush.

Sloshing through the garden and to and from the hotel was a misery, and, having become warm in centrally heated rooms, we had to plunge out into the raw dampness outside and then stay for hours in a chilly, draughty house.

No wonder that *Mademoiselle* succumbed to the dread influenza germ and had to go to bed. Then followed a hectic time for me. I had to nurse my patient in the hotel, rush across to our *depôt* to receive visitors, and give out supplies ; cook for, exercise, and then dry the dogs ; pound back again to the hotel to put anti-phlogistine mud on *Mademoiselle*, then hurry back to the house. A nightmare time of anxiety.

When she had recovered enough to return to work (*Mademoiselle*, being *Mademoiselle*, of course got up too soon), officers were coming every day to the *depôt*. I, personally, delivered the wherewithal to furnish three new *foyers* up in the mountains, and always I was struck by the morale of officers and men. In one lonely village on the frontier I was conducted to the Colonel's quarters in a tumble-down farmhouse. I sploshed through the morass of mud and manure, between high banks of soft mud-stained snow recently scraped away to form a pathway for the men. Outside the main door, to amuse themselves in their free time, the soldiers had made a wooden cannon.

The Colonel's room was the hay-loft and its furniture a camp-bed, a rickety wooden chair, and a deal table strewn with papers. The first floor was used as an *Infirmerie*, in which a few soldiers with coughs and colds were rolled in blankets and lying upon trusses of straw around a central stove. The kitchen of the farmhouse was used as the officers' mess-room, and the men slept in the stables and outhouses.

Our packages were received with delight, especially the gramophone, and the Colonel led me to a cow-byre where several happy, whistling soldiers were frantically scraping manure and stained whitewash from the walls before whitening them once more, for this was to be their *foyer*. The officers, to inspire their men, were hard at work making a little *foyer* for themselves, as the kitchen, when the evening meal was over, became an overflow-infirmary for a few delicate *poilus* who could sleep on the floor before the fire. As the men, tired after their long days of work, went to bed very early, the officers had, then, nowhere to sit. So they were converting a small outhouse into a *foyer* for themselves, and doing it very beautifully. It had high wooden tables with legs formed by birch logs, with the silvery-grey bark left upon them. High stools were made of round slices of tree-trunks supported by tripods of silver birch. In a corner of the shed they had pieced together silvery logs, making a *capote* over an imaginary fireplace, to give the illusion of the fire they lacked. Fans of silver bark in each corner of the room, near the ceiling, shielded lit candles and gave a lovely effect of hidden radiance.

When I came in, the regimental artist was drawing bold sketches of mountain ranges, snow-peaks, and ski-ers with coloured chalks upon large sheets of grey packing-paper. These were to be nailed upon the planked walls to serve as decoration—and also as draught-screens. " *C'est coquet, notre foyer, Madame ?* " laughed a young officer. And, indeed, it was.

CHAPTER VI.

MORALE.

As I drove down that bleak precipitous road, between desolate pine-woods sighing in the icy wind, meeting for miles no other car, not even a stray peasant, not even a wandering dog, I marvelled at those men, quartered in that squalid isolated village, making for themselves something out of nothing to keep up their spirits and to occupy their leisure time. And I thought of the wonderful remark of a *coiffeur* in Cannes, whom one day I found digging fiercely in an abandoned plot of ground at the back of the shop. Business was slack; for many English and American clients had hurried home, and so he had decided to keep up the morale of the staff by making all the pretty little manicurists and *coiffeuses* do some hard gardening while awaiting customers. Nicole was energetically delving with a trowel to displace some self-sown plants which Monsieur Edmond had discovered. Elise was collecting stones from the newly turned earth; Marcelle was raking it over; Yvonne was watering the plants, herself, and the other squealing workers, with a hose. All were chattering like magpies and as happy as larks. For the time they had forgotten that they were living under a cloud of anxiety for the fate of fathers, brothers, *fiancés*, and husbands. They looked so pretty flitting about that abandoned garden in their white overalls.

"So you are making a garden," I said, and the girls laughed and started patting their curls and washing soil-begrimed hands under the tap. Monsieur Edmond straightened his bent back, and, sweeping a feather of grey hair out of his eyes, said cheerfully—

"*Madame, quand tout le monde detruit, il faut construire.*"

Well, those soldiers on a peak of the High Alps were doing the same thing. All over France men and women were doing constructive work while the engines of war destroyed. That was then the spirit of France. I felt very proud of the French Army as I drove down that mountain road; as proud of them as I had felt when, two summers ago, *Mademoiselle* and I had watched the President review the Alpine troops at Le Lautaret.

We had driven, in one day, from the Midi to our *bergerie*, perched on a plateau facing the Meije glacier, and had reached our destination tired out. We were told that although the Review would not begin until ten o'clock next morning, the roads would be closed to traffic at 7 A.M. Horrible thought! Had we enough energy left to breakfast at 5 A.M. next day after such a journey?

We decided that the effort must be made
—and we made it. I shall ever be thankful
that we did, for I would not have missed so
wonderful a sight for all the world. We
cunningly placed ourselves on a slope just
below the P.L.M. Hotel and behind (and above)
the enclosure where the President and officials
would stand. From this point we commanded
the complete panorama. For two hours the
troops marched, or rode at the gallop, past
the President. They were magnificent men.
There were *Chasseurs Alpins* in their smart
dark blue uniforms and jaunty *bérets;* there
were Zouaves, there were Senegalese, there
were the Moroccan troops, and, most picturesque
of all, the Spahis, mounted upon superb white
Arab horses. They galloped down the Galibier
full tilt, their scarlet cloaks billowing behind
them. It made one quite breathless to see
them coming down that steep and dangerous
mountain road; to hear the thundering of
their approach.

Soon after we had taken our place on the
side of the mountain I had remarked to
Mademoiselle—

" Look ! The wild rhododendrons are out !
I can see a red patch of them right up at the
very top of the Galibier."

Mademoiselle had turned her field-glasses upon
my far-distant patch of rhododendrons—

" It's the Spahis waiting there," she said,
" you see their red cloaks."

We were in a marvellous position; for we

overlooked a view of all the main roads, which became rivers of troops flowing down from the Galibier to Le Lautaret, then diverging towards Briançon to the left and La Grave to the right, the whole scene framed by the majestic snow-peaks of the High Alps.

Tanks rumbled past us, armoured cars; motor-bicycles with side-cars, armed with miniature guns; the heavy guns; the light artillery; the divine Newfoundland dogs with their Red Cross outfits strapped to their backs; more ambulances; every most modern contrivance of war, even to a gyroplane which circled above us and made miraculous vertical descents.

We loved the regimental mascots. There was a glossy goat, and innumerable dogs left their regiments at intervals to race across the flower-starred grass, returning and falling in with the soldiers for the march past the President. We stood there watching this wonderful military pageant, listening to the music of regimental bands, the drone of aeroplanes overhead, the thunder and roar of motor transport, and I thrilled to think that we were seeing only twenty thousand of the six or seven million men that France could mobilise if war broke out. This was only the Alpine Army.

We had been much intrigued by important people, wearing the exclusive badge which entitled them to sit in the enclosure with the President, escaping from it and walking across to a jutting corner of the mountain some dis-

tance beyond us. We wondered if this could
be a better spot from which to witness the
review, but we decided to stay ; for we were
so well-placed and the mob was so dense. Nevertheless, we asked ourselves what could be
hidden behind that promontory of rock.

And what do you think it was ? Afterwards
we were told. It was a group of wounded
war veterans, officers who had fought in the
war of 1914. They were too old, or too maimed,
to climb the height of the Galibier, and so
were hidden inside this bend so that when
their regiments passed that corner they could
fall in, unseen, and march past their President
in the place of honour at the head of their
regiment. We had seen them pass, some
limping, some disfigured, all with tunics covered
with faded ribbons, and that sight had broken
us both down, for they looked so tired and
so proud, yet so sad. No doubt they were
thinking, as we were, that these thousands of
splendid young men who marched with them
might, some day soon, be dead or mangled
in the horrors of another war. They themselves
would be too old to fight ; their day was done.
But these keen and glorious boys . . .?

One last experience you must share with me.

It is Christmas Eve in one of the many
foyers we have by this time installed in the
High Alps. Picture a huge derelict barn.
The soldiers have covered gaping voids in
its walls with brown paper and sacks to keep
out the snow. Upon a great stove, glowing

red-hot in its centre, steams a mighty *marmite* filled with hot spiced wine. Deal trestle tables are ranged in lines along the length of the floor, covered at intervals with brightly coloured squares of American cloth—the shiny side is used when hot drinks are being served, and when the men play *belote* they turn the squares fluffy-side uppermost so that the cards do not slip. Wooden benches are drawn up to the tables, and camp-stools, with seats of multi-coloured striped canvas, are ranged around the stove. The dim planked sides of the barn are hung with strips of flowered cretonne (odd lengths sent by some kind French shopkeeper, in case they might be useful), with paper festoons, and coloured chalk sketches, to hide the improvised snow-screens of sacking. In the most conspicuous place are hung the Allied flags, touchingly entwined.

A glistening pine tree stands in a corner, and at its foot, half-hidden under the dark branches, the soldiers have arranged a little *crèche*, peopled with brown-cloaked shepherds and gaudy kings; the humble of heart bringing presents of bread and wine; a stiff, standing St Joseph, a blue-clad Virgin, kneeling beside a straw-filled manger wherein lies a very pink Holy Baby, modelled, because He represents the Christ-Child, in wax, whereas His encircling adorers are carved, roughly, in wood. The beasts are there, too, of course; the patient oxen lying down close to the manger so that their breath may warm the Holy Child; the

overladen ass, resting awhile ; the black cock
that signalled the betrayer, crowing on a
branch. Some peasant has lent a large, plump,
waxen angel, swathed in spangled blue. This
precious possession is suspended from a wire
above the *crèche*, dwarfing into Lilliputian
dimensions the figures within it.

All along the sides of the barn straw, thickly
strewn, forms a sleeping-place for many soldiers,
and the muffled breathing, stamping and
snorting of cows and stabled mules near-by,
gives one the illusion of a huge *crèche* enfolding
a tiny one.

The scene is lit by shepherds' lanterns and
packed with soldiers from wall to wall, some
playing cards, some playing *loto*, draughts,
dominoes, or chess ; others licking pencil-points
as they laboriously indite letters to their
families ; a studious few reading books ; a
more frivolous majority joking over the illustrated magazines ; a reverent group crouching
over the *crèche* and discussing the figures therein ;
and a musician, seated upon the corner of a
table, playing the accordion. All are cheerful
and content.

No one is touching the spiced wine. Why ?
Because all are going to the Midnight Mass
to be held in the little ancient church of stone
built high upon that snow-clad mountain peak.
Afterwards those soldiers will return to their
beloved *foyer* and will celebrate Christmas Day.

Presently they all file out into the icy air,
into the hard bright moonlight, and climb up

steep stone stairways, covered deep with frozen snow, upon which the black shadows of queer old houses are sharply defined. Here and there, high up in a crazy gable, a candle burns in a window ; the deep music of the church bell rings out its summons to the Midnight Mass and echoes around the majestic snow-clad mountains.

Inside the little church is warmth and a blaze of light from a myriad candles. Again one sees a *crèche*, in an alcove of the chancel. Every plaster saint is garlanded and illumined ; the regimental band of the *Chasseurs Alpins* is playing a Christmas hymn. A soldier-priest then sings the Mass. It is startling to hear a voice of such depth, and range, and purity of tone in so remote a place, and its beauty unmans some of the soldiers. The priest addresses the men as " *Mes camarades, mes frères*," he speaks of the personal *foyers* they have left, and bids them be sure that God will have them in His keeping, His soldier sons and their beloved families which, for the sake of *la Patrie*, they have left. Then he walks down the chancel steps, followed by small scarlet acolytes carrying unsteady tapers ; takes the image of the Holy Child from its cradle and carries it back to the altar. There he stands facing the congregation, holding out the Baby in his arms, while soldier after soldier files up to the altar to kiss its hand, its foot, its robe, as an act of adoration.

Then they all sing a joyful Christmas hymn, and, after the final benediction, they troop out into the cold moonlight once more, back to their *foyer*, where they drink to each other, and to the success of the Allies, the victory of *La France* and *l'Angleterre*, in the hot spiced wine.

In the morning a dog-team, drawing a sledge laden with Christmas letters and parcels, races to the foot of the mountain, and soldiers on skis skim down upon it like great wheeling birds, and carry those sacks of joy back to their *foyer*.

We will leave the men to their happiness. . . .

When I left the snows, and came home again to little 'Sunset House,' I found a pile of letters awaiting me, and among them one from a young Lieutenant who had lodged with me during the first hectic weeks of the war when all our houses were filled to overflowing with French soldiers. This boy recalled the peace of my garden on warm moonlit nights and the scent of roses and jasmin which drifted into my windows. His last words touched me very deeply—

"*Notre bref séjour chez vous, Madame, ne fut-il pas le trait-d'union idéal entre la douceur des foyers que nous venions de quitter et l'inconnu de notre destin ?*"

Well, if in our own houses, and in our FOYERS DES SOLDATS DE FRANCE, we could make these men feel a little less lonely and lost ; if we could change their sad thoughts and give them at least some of the cosiness and comfort of their own homes ; soften, even in a small degree, the bitterness of those separations— then our work was very well worth while.

CHAPTER VII.

ENERVATION.

ANYONE who has descended, in one day, from the pure icy atmosphere of the High Alps in winter to the comparative warmth of the South of France will doubtless have felt like a boned chicken before it has been restuffed, or an orange that has had all its vital juices savagely sucked from it by a greedy child. *Mademoiselle*, my neighbour of the Château, and I, both suffered from that lotus-lassitude for the first few days of our return. She had scarcely yet recovered from the dread form of influenza which she had contracted in Briançon. We had both worked very hard under rather severe and adverse conditions, rendered bearable, however, by the pathetic gratitude of the officers and men whose hard lot we were trying to soften.

Now that our work was *in train*, we could think of some hundreds of soldiers of the Alpine Army comforted by the warm woollen clothing we had been able to provide, made from wool bought from the peasants of the mountains, to be knitted into socks, snow-helmets, and

mufflers by soldiers' wives to whom we had
ensured paid employment throughout the
winter.

We could picture those men drinking hot
coffee or chocolate, playing draughts or *belote*
or chess, writing letters to their families, reading
French books and magazines, playing their
wireless, or gramophone, or accordion in the
fifty-seven *foyers* we had already established ;
and we were entitled to a short period of
rest.

In war-time, however, no one can rest at all
in mind, and very seldom in body. The need
of the men in the High Alps was urgent and,
so far, we had only catered for the comfort
of a very small proportion of those twenty
thousand soldiers. More and more *foyers* must
be created behind the lines, and, later on,
Mademoiselle wanted to provide mobile canteens
and disinfecting vans, with douches, for soldiers
in the front line. She remembered the misery
of the men to whom she had ministered during
the war of 1914-18 who had lacked these
things.

But what we lacked, now, was money. When
we rushed up to the High Alps, *Mademoiselle*
had her personal Bank account and I, luckily,
had just received a fat cheque of advance
royalties for my new book, just published.

With these monies we had met our initial
outlays, and, when we had spent all we had,
we still continued recklessly (as some thought)
to order thousands of woollen comforts, of

medicaments, for the little *Postes de Secours*, and of games for our *foyers*. We knew that money would come from somewhere, must come—for our faith, and the need of the soldiers, were so great. But, for the moment, our money was spent.

Mademoiselle, crouching before the huge fireplace of her sitting-room (once the Monks' kitchen, for her Château was, in olden days, a Monastery), formulated schemes for raising money to help her beloved soldiers. Or she prowled about her old dim house with her lithe Indian walk, her great haunted eyes seeing visions of horror to come—the repetition of horrors she had seen before and ever after striven, vainly, to forget. She could not rest. At moments, tired as she was, she would scourge herself and those around her into feverish activity. I was lashed up our mountain by the whip of her tongue to pen propaganda in my little ' Sunset House ' for private circulation among our friends in America ; I was commanded to accept every social invitation I received and to interest everybody I met in our work for the French Army ; I must see that my gardener cultivated every corner of my property in preparation for spring sowing so that each of our houses might be self-supporting and our surplus vegetables supply needy peasants during the hard time to come. Once again we were all working, under easier conditions, certainly, but working strenuously all the same. We had no rest at all.

And then, suddenly, the weather changed.
One morning I was awakened by a sensation
of warmth and weight upon my shoulder and
something nuzzling close under my chin. It
was Dominie, my little Blackness. Feeling
cold, he had forsaken his cushion on the floor
beside my bed and was cuddling just as close
to me as he could get, his nose pushed under
my chin and his great cocker ears spread over
my chest. Amber eyes looked apologetically
into mine as they opened. He was shivering.
The ceiling was barred with a cold blue light
filtering through the slats of the shutters.
Snow-glare—I had grown accustomed to that
queer ghostly light in the High Alps—snow
must have fallen in the night. Indeed it had.
The shape of my terraced garden was completely obliterated and my flowers buried by
it. Here and there the surface of the white
sea of snow was broken by cypress trees bent
almost double with its weight, and by a scrawl
of broken telephone and electric wires which
had not withstood the strain of this un-
accustomed load. When Dominie went out
for his early morning run he came back to me
with banner ears, feathered legs, and floppy
feet caked with hard frozen snow which took
me and his devoted slave, my *bonne* (who, to
my joy, returned to me when Italy did not
declare war against France), a quarter of an
hour to remove and, for the first time, he
did not bring me his daily bouquet of flowers
which she always picked for him to carry back

to me in that velvet mouth of his. Everything was buried in snow. Outside my garage it was over a metre deep. Impossible to get out my car, or for any car to approach my house.

This was the 31st of December. I spent my New Year's Eve alone with Dominie by my fireside, writing letters by candlelight. Impossible to attend any New Year festivities next day. I was imprisoned in my little fort and, the telephone wires having been broken, quite unable to communicate with the outside world. But I had great fun, wading thigh-deep in my garden, liberating my poor cypress trees bent almost double with the load of snow. This, in the Midi. The strangeness of it all.

I mention this fall of snow, so extraordinary in the South of France, because, beside cutting our communication with the outside world, it also complicated our lives and plunged us into drifts of new work, deeper than the snow-drifts. For, the moment they could get to us, came officers of the reserve troops stationed in the villages of the neighbourhood, praying for *foyers* for their men who were lodged in draughty barns and sleeping on the cement floors of garages; and for shelter for their horses, which were tethered under olive trees and dying from exposure because every stable and outhouse was already crammed with soldiers. The lot of the men was pitiful now that the world was covered with this unnatural blanket of snow; until now they had fared very well in the warm sunshine of the Midi. We were told that there was a spirit of grumbling and discontent among them. Most of them came from the coast towns and inland villages of the Var; the scum of Marseilles and Toulon had, of course, been mobilised with the better men and now was floating on the top, contaminating the loyal peasants who make the strong red wine of France. Could we give each batallion a warm *foyer* of its own where the men could shelter from the cold and amuse themselves? Their *morale* must be kept up. We protested that we were collecting funds to help the Alpine Army which was in much harder case, and we pointed out that the men of the Midi could reach inns and *cafés* and little restaurants, which did not exist in the High Alps. We were told that this was the one thing the officers wanted to prevent. In the local inns and *cafés* the men were given drink and Communist propaganda was pushed into their pockets. It was most urgent that they should have *foyers*.

So the rot of Communism had tainted the army of the South. In the Alps we had found the *morale* of the men magnificent. Never a murmur of discontent or self-pity under conditions of real hardship. All were hard and loyal, enduring this long wait for something to happen with patience and cheerful confidence.

During the weeks that followed, *Mademoiselle*

and I, in moments of discouragement, had constantly to lift up our eyes and hearts to those icy majestic peaks that we had left.

"These are only reservists, grown soft, and men who have seen no service, Peg," she would remind me. "Think of those hard, splendid officers and men up in the High Alps, and those we had with us at first. They represent the real French Army."

We had already supplied a *foyer* in our own village and a young Lieutenant was detailed to superintend it and to appoint non-commissioned officers to see that the men kept it clean. But, when we visited it, we generally found the floor littered with empty cigarette *cartons*, dead matches, stumps of cigarettes, straw, and stable dung. One could write one's name in the coating of dust collected on the top of the gramophone cabinet I had given to the men; packets of playing cards, supplied for their amusement, and books from their library had mysteriously disappeared—and never reappeared—and we found that the generous supply of coffee, sugar, and chocolate, which should have comforted the men for months, had all been used up in a fortnight. The *chef*, to whom the store had been confided, had been giving it to the men for breakfast, then again during the mornings and afternoons (as well as their Army ration) instead of only at night when the *foyer* was open. We could not blame the men; for private soldiers, all the world over, are but schoolboys, greedy, thoughtless, and untidy until they are taught better. It was entirely the fault of the officers who, bored with military inaction (as Hitler intended they should be), only tried to alleviate their own boredom instead of interesting themselves in the welfare and discipline of their men. They were, with some good exceptions, a soft, lazy lot.

I had my first glimpse of this when some of them visited me and asked if, as I had so kindly housed so many officers and soldiers at the beginning of the war, I would again take in a guest or two. In France, the law is that no woman, living alone, shall have soldiers billeted in her house, and that no foreigner can be compelled to take in the military. But at the moment of General Mobilisation, we, of the little English Colony, had thrown wide the doors of our houses, garages, stables, and even potting-sheds to shelter some of the eighteen hundred soldiers who were vainly trying to find lodging in a tiny mountain village of but three hundred inhabitants. The situation, now, was very different. Italy had not come into the war as had then been anticipated; the splendid troops that had come to us, in relays, had been moved up North, to the Alpine forts and those of the Maginot Line; we had now only one *Groupe* of Heavy Artillery in our village and other *groupes*, of the same regiment, scattered in neighbouring villages; and there were many empty houses of English, Americans, and even French, who

had fled just before war was declared. Any
of these could be commandeered by the Army,
but the officers very naturally preferred the
comfort of inhabited dwellings where hot baths
could be had at all hours and the rooms were
warmed. As there was no longer need to give
hospitality in my own house, I offered my little
garage flat which I had recently built and
decorated. It had a bedroom with two divan
beds, a sitting-room, bathroom, and a kitchen
equipped with a gas-cooker and a frigidaire.
It stood in its own paved courtyard and was
situated about a hundred yards from my house,
approached by a stone stairway overgrown
with flowers—rather a lovely little secret place
which had already been the delight of former
French officers.

I conducted thither the two sleek Lieutenants
who had asked me to take them in. They
expressed their admiration for its situation
and installation, but said that of course the
flat would only do for *one* of them. If two of
them shared a room, one would inevitably
disturb the other if he went to bed later, or
got up earlier ; and then it was very distasteful
to share a bathroom with anyone.

This, from men who would soon be living
in muddy or snow-filled trenches by day and
sleeping in dug-outs by night (the sooner the
better, I thought).

My *bonne* and I, therefore, made up one of
the two beds, and soon afterwards a fat and
forty-ish Lieutenant occupied it. I was much

irritated, a week later, when his orderly came down with a request from Lieutenant X. that the other bed in his room should be made up immediately as the veterinary surgeon of the battalion was returning from his leave that night and had no lodging arranged. My annoyance was a little tempered by the fact that I liked the Vet. very much. He really worried about the sick horses and mules under his care, always striving to stable them better ; and, before he went on leave, he had very kindly come in to advise me upon some puppy-ailment of Dominie. But my annoyance flared into real anger when, ten days later, I received a charming postcard from my friend the Vet., written from his home in Northern France, inquiring for the health of my little Blackness and telling me that he was in luck for his leave had been extended for a month. . . .

Who, then, was sharing my flat with that fat middle-aged Lieutenant ?

A visit there soon explained the mystery. Officers do not wear *crêpe-de-Chine* night-dresses. . . . Then I fairly boiled. Abuse of hospitality and, far worse, infraction of military regulations by an officer who had not hesitated to send down his orderly with a lie to his hostess. That orderly had the care of the flat. What opinion could he have of his officer ? Neither officers nor men were allowed to have their wives with them—and this Lieutenant was unmarried.

My first impulse was to go straight to the

Commandant of the regiment and make a h—l
of a row, but upon reflection I decided to
manage the affair myself. I wrote a polite
letter to Lieutenant X. regretting that I should
require my flat the next day for my own use.

He departed, and I received three sheets
of fulsome thanks for all my kindness written
upon mauve-tinted scented notepaper which,
however, did not stink in my nostrils as highly
as did this incident.

Later, I was asked by the Commandant
if I would consent to be *marraine* to the second
Groupe of his regiment ; three hundred men,
stationed in a lovely little hill-town (once
described as " the little town of dreams and
deep sweet bells ") not very far away. These
men had no amenities whatever. I had seen
them sitting shivering on walls, kicking the
snow from their boots and smoking *caporal*
cigarettes or squatting on straw near their
quarters, playing *belote* in the evenings by
the light of a candle. My neighbour, Mrs
Phillips Oppenheim, reported to me that she
had seen a soldier sitting on a log in a snow-
covered field, writing a letter upon the circular
top of a wine barrel which he had nailed to a
post as an improvised desk.

" I should like to do something for the men
quartered near our house," she said. " Could
I make them a little *foyer* on the plan of those
you've been installing in the High Alps ? How
do I set about it ? " We made lists of necessaries
and, financed enthusiastically by her author-

husband, we made shopping expeditions, until one day her little *foyer* was opened with military honours and sweet champagne, and she became *marraine* of the soldiers on her property.

I was instituted *marraine* of three hundred god-sons in " the little town of dreams " and decorated by the Commandant with the *ensigne* of the regiment to the strains of the Marseillaise, and then—he asked me if I could, perhaps, create a *foyer* for my *filleuls*. Knowing well the cost of such an enterprise, my spirit quailed a bit. I had already spent nearly all my personal money and I knew that *Mademoiselle* could not help me. Our funds had run out, as I have said, and she had many more requests for *foyers* for the High Alps which she had promised to fulfil as soon as she could. I must just earn some money by writing; my god-sons must have their *foyer*. The dear old Mayor of the little hill-town was enchanted that someone would help him with the problem of cold and discontented soldiers. He eagerly offered me a huge abandoned room over the *Mairie* for my *foyer*. It lacked panes in the enormous arched windows, it lacked furniture, in fact it lacked everything save space, and of that there was enough to house, if necessary, five hundred men at a time. It was a very beautiful room.

With a pulse that beat rather unevenly, for it was a big undertaking to render that room habitable, I asked the Commandant to appoint an officer who would superintend the installation of the *foyer* and run it, afterwards, for the men. I was given a Lieutenant and I empowered him to order glass for the windows, and wood for tables and benches, which I suggested should be made by the carpenter of the *Groupe*, also electric wire and fittings, and to send the bills to me. I told him that I, myself, would buy a gramophone and discs, games, notepaper, books and magazines when the room was ready. He professed zeal and promised to telephone to me when all was prepared.

The civilians of that little town were mad keen to help me. The village schoolmistress supplied me with a stove for the *foyer ;* someone suggested a raffle to raise funds for it ; the Mayor importuned the few more affluent residents for subscriptions—only the Lieutenant detailed to me was apathetic.

When, for more than a fortnight, I had had no message from him announcing that the work on the room was finished, and all efforts to communicate with him by the now re-established telephone had failed, in desperation I donned my ski-ing costume and climbed through the snow up to the little town of dreams. I found that room in exactly the same state as I had left it. Wind blew in through gaping windows and eddied wisps of straw and clouds of dust around its dismal emptiness. Nothing whatever had been done in the interval.

Raging internally, I ploughed my way home again through the snow, stopped at intervals

by groups of my god-sons who asked me,
pathetically, when their *foyer* would be open.

In the end I was obliged to tour the country
to find glass and wood, and then workmen to
make nine large tables and eighteen benches.
Wood had all been commandeered by the
Army and the village carpenters were all serving.
It was necessary to rout out the Commandant
and get him to give me the regimental carpenters. Never in my life have I met a more
helpless or more incompetent youth than that
Lieutenant. When I asked for him to be replaced
by something alive, his substitute almost
immediately went on leave, and so it went on
after the *foyer* was, at last, opened. It was an
exasperating time.

No one officer was ever responsible for that
foyer, but fortunately the N.C.O.'s were good
and keen, so that it was kept tolerably clean
and the *poilus* were immensely proud of it.

When, during this exasperating time, I sometimes went down to the Château to let off
steam to *Mademoiselle*, she looked at me with
the same disillusionment in her eyes that she
must have seen in mine, and said : " Don't
be discouraged, Pegs. It is quite, quite awful.
But remember those splendid men who were
here at the beginning of the war—remember
those we have left in the High Alps. Do what
you can for these *men*—and try to forget their
officers."

One other experience I will chronicle—for
at least it made me laugh.

A young doctor, of another regiment stationed a few miles away, came to crave the hospitality of my garage-flat, for he was billeted in an unspeakably dirty hovel. He planned to make an *Infirmerie*, for men not sick enough to be sent to hospital yet needing first-aid treatment, in a partially abandoned farm-house just across my lane. If I would permit him to occupy my flat, he would always be near his *malades*. Of course I consented, and it was arranged that he should take up his residence there in a week's time.

Two nights later, I was writing, very late at night, in my Studio when, to my startled consternation, I heard a tremendous babel of raucous shouting which seemed to come from somewhere in my property. Yells and shouts of men tore the dark stillness. What could be happening? It sounded as though the whole French Army, in a drunken condition, had invaded my little *domaine*. Carefully veiling my light (for the black-out regulations were very strict), I cautiously opened the door leading into the garden and peered out. To my horror I saw a blaze of light surrounding my garage-flat, built upon the highest and most conspicuous point of my property. That noise *must* emanate from the throats of drunken soldiers who had broken through the boundary fence and taken possession.

This must be looked into. Dominie, heckles up, was growling nervously in the most comfortable chair, feeling that he ought to do something about it, but obviously hoping that no call would be made upon him. He rolled an apprehensive eye upon me as I fastened on his lead and seized a poker from the fireplace. He realised that he was to be dragged (literally) into this affair.

Together we climbed the long stone stairway and opened the door which led into the private courtyard of the garage-flat. To my surprise —and relief—it was deserted. The blaze of light and the mad shouting issued from the unshuttered bedroom windows. Approaching stealthily, I looked in. Instead of a drunken crowd of soldiery, I saw one solitary little man, clad in loud mauve-striped pyjamas, smoking a cigarette, and listening to a small portable wireless. I remembered, then, that Hitler was to make his great speech that night. The yells that I heard were those of German youths, intoxicated by the eloquence of their Führer.

And the little man was the doctor, who had decided to move to more comfortable quarters immediately, but had omitted to inform his hostess of his sudden change of plans.

Keeping behind a sheltering shutter so that he should feel less embarrassed, I tapped peremptorily upon the window and called " *Docteur ! Docteur !* "

There was an immediate silence. He had switched off the wireless and was listening. I announced myself and told him of the scare that he had given me, and he opened the window a crack to pour forth a voluble explanation of his presence there before the date arranged. Having seen this little Paradise, he could not rest until he had taken possession. It was, of course, most reprehensible that he had not apprised *Madame* of his change of plans—but it was a sudden impulse——

I cut him short by suggesting that I should close the shutters for him (they fastened from outside), whereupon he implored me not to deprive him of the beautiful stars and the lovely soft lines of the mountains seen dimly against that starlit sky.

I reminded him that as I was a landed proprietor I should be heavily fined if any light were apparent on my property. Whereupon he exclaimed: *" Mon Dieu! j'avais complêtement oublié que nous sommes en guerre."* . . .

I wanted to remark that he was not the only officer in the neighbourhood who seemed to have completely forgotten that we were at war.

CHAPTER VIII.

THE RED TARE.

SMALL wonder that the seed of Communism, planted and manured so well by the Blum Government, still sprouted in the hearts of certain discontented *poilus*. The self-indulgence of this section of Army officers and their entire neglect of the welfare of the soldiers under their command gave the men a just grievance and soured them against all those in better case than they. In my heart I knew that if I had to clean the military boots of that fat Lieutenant who had occupied my flat, with hate in my heart I should probably smear them with mud or paint the legend *Liberté! Egalité! Fraternité!* ironically upon them. Those officers were enough to turn the staunchest patriot into a raging Bolshevik.

That wind of Communism which had swept Northern France had blown, also, among our mountains of the Midi and had even ruffled us. I had engaged a young boy of sixteen to help in my garden, and, at the moment of *Mobilisation Générale* when, as in England, every householder was told to clear their lofts and attics of junk, I had climbed up into my *grenier* one afternoon to do this distasteful job. As I stacked and cleared out cardboard boxes and all things inflammable, I handed down these materials for a very good bonfire to the boy who was standing on the ladder below me. "Don't light that bonfire now," I enjoined him, "it would go on burning like a beacon far into the night and we should get into trouble with the military" (my house was then full of French officers of the best type).

To my astonishment and disgust, the boy, hitherto very polite, gave me an impudent grin and remarked pertly with a sneering smile : "You *are* afraid of getting into trouble with the military, aren't you ?" For the first time, he had omitted to remove his cap on entering my house and he stood before me with it worn well on one side, the peak pulled low over one insolent eye, his hands on his hips in a swaggering attitude while he chewed a bit of grass. I dismissed him next day.

Anyone who has lived, as I have been privileged to do, among the French peasantry with their perfect natural courtesy, will realise how startled I was by this behaviour in one of the younger generation. The Communistic spirit pervaded all the youths of every village. *Mademoiselle* suffered much from one who, wearing a scarlet pullover (the popular colour at that time), was posted as a spy on the wall at the foot of the approach to her Château and who tried to prevent anyone going to

work on her property. There were paid
agitators in every hamlet, and the Communist
sign was painted everywhere on signposts, walls,
and the doors of barns.

Messieurs Daladier and Reynaud made a
crusade against Communism and certain Communistic Deputies even suffered imprisonment,
but a thing suppressed is not necessarily killed,
and during those last months I lived in the
South of France I was always coming across
evidence that the subtle poison was still being
administered to simple folk whose lot in life
was hard. A *poilu* to whom I was talking in
my *foyer* one evening, asked me if I did not
think it was a scandal that his wife only had
eight francs a day Government allowance
whereas an officer's wife had eight thousand
a week. I was staggered. I assured him that
officers' wives received no allowance at all.
He shook his head dubiously, gave me a glance
of suspicion, shrugged his shoulders, and slouched
away, obviously unconvinced.

When one of our great Generals from G.H.Q.
(B.E.F.) came to see me, he told me that our
Foyers des Soldats de France were immensely
important. He said that the British soldier
was so well paid in comparison to the French,
who only got 50 centimes a day; that our
Army was so tiny in comparison to the French
millions that our men were inundated with
comforts and cigarettes, provided with wonderful
canteens and clubs; their hospitals and First
Aid posts supplied with masses of medical

stores and every possible surgical appliance even to ' iron lungs ' and wonderful ambulances, which, for so huge an army as the French, were impossible. He said that now the English and the French were one large family and that it was wrong that certain members of it should be spoiled and others go lacking.

" I shall send you some of our surplus English cigarettes for your *poilus*," he said. Which he afterwards did, to their great pride and delight.

The French police, all over France, were growing very jumpy and suspicious. They evidently knew of Fifth Column activities, and at one time were trying to track cars which travelled round with wireless transmitters and receivers hid within them. One was detected and caught in our region. Rumours of the activities of spies abounded and even I, an innocent member of the English Colony, who had worked for the French Army since the outbreak of the war, came under the suspicion of the Police. It was in this wise.

My other dear neighbour possessed a much beloved dog named Sophy, whom she adored. Sophy had been her companion for many years and had grown both blind and deaf. *Mademoiselle* dreaded the moment when dear old ' Sos,' as we sometimes called Sophy, must leave us, and she made me promise that if this should happen when she (*Mademoiselle*) was away from home, that I would immediately send her a telegram. She had known Sophy's

mistress for many years and realised that she
would break her heart in silence rather than
talk of her grief to a comparative newcomer
(myself). *Mademoiselle* insisted that she must
be there to share such a sorrow.

It did so happen that this tragedy befell us
while *Mademoiselle* was away. She had gone
up to our *depôt* in Briançon, taking with her
a new volunteer and more stores and equipment
for old, and new, *foyers* that we were still
installing in the High Alps. I felt reluctant
to distress her while she was doing such important work, but I remembered that promise
made long ago. And so, after that sad visit
of the Vet., I telephoned the following telegram
to the General Post Office in Grasse—

" *Rozier est venu ce matin faire endormir Sophy.*"

(Rozier (the Vet.) came this morning to put
    Sophy to sleep.)

I remember asking the telephone operator
how best to express the fact that a dog had
had to be put away—what word should I
use ? " *Piqué,*" was his reply. " But if I say
that, my friend will only think that the dog
has had an injection " (*piqure,* in French) I
objected. " I want her to know the truth."
He told me, rather crossly, to say what I liked,
and so I used the verbs *faire endormir*.

Having performed my promise I thought
no more of that telegram. Sophy's mistress,
looking like someone who has been suddenly

stabbed, nevertheless behaved with her usual courage ; visited the *foyer* in our village and even drove with me to Cannes for dinner and to see a film next day. *Mademoiselle* came home at the end of the week and life resumed its war-time course. None of us ever again spoke of that curly black companion, with her funny ways, who had so endeared herself to us all.

Weeks passed, and one morning my *bonne* brought me a long envelope with a government stamp. It was from the Chief of Police in Cannes, asking me to present myself at his office without fail at 10 A.M. the next day to speak of a private matter concerning myself. WHAT had I done ? How transgressed the French laws ? Could this concern my employment of an Italian *bonne ?* I tried to recall any sin of omission or commission that I might have perpetrated against the French State, but, having a clear conscience at that moment, this police summons left me entirely bewildered. I went down to Cannes next day, feeling incredibly nervous. I had always been friends with the French police in Grasse. I had been a member of their *Amicale* Society for years. I did not want this comfortable relationship to be upset, especially in war-time.

I was ushered by a very solemn *gendarme* into a cold cell-like room which was the Chief's office. There he sat, a most terrifying individual with a tremendous black, up-curled moustache and lowering brows. Without speaking he

motioned me to the only other chair, with the
light glaring upon my face. I was determined
not to speak until he did ; to ask no questions
and to answer his without heat, however
infuriating they might be. It was infuriating,
already, to be received as though I were a
criminal, weary as I was in the service of this
man's Army.

He still sat, in silence, turning over page
after page of what I supposed must be my
dossier, occasionally shooting at me a glance
of dark suspicion from under partially lowered
lids. I wanted to scream, or to throw something
at him ; to say something insulting or—and
more than all—to light a cigarette. Of course
I did none of these things. Instead, I said to
myself, " Two can play at this dumb game.
I won't speak until I'm spoken to."

After what seemed an interminable age this
silence of intimidation was at last broken.
It had had its effect ; for my first indignation
had gradually evaporated and I was reduced
to a chilly state of nervous apprehension.

I was asked the names of my father and
mother.

Of what nationality were they ?

Were they still living ?

When did they die—and where ?

What was my father's profession ?

I was, apparently (he consulted my *dossier*),
a widow.

When did my husband die ?

Where ?

How old was he when he died ?

What was his profession ? (My information on this point seemed to shake him a little.)

When did he come to France ?

Where did we live ?

What did we pay for our property ?

How much income had my husband ?

From what sources did it come ?

How much did he leave me at his death ?

Where did I live now ?

What had I done with my former property ?

How much had I paid for my cottage in Opio ?

These appalling questions went on and on, but still I refrained, by a gigantic effort, from asking him what it was all about.

When the personal *questionnaire* was over, and it took a very long time because all my answers had to be written down, my passport was demanded and the journeys of years noted and every visa for every foreign country carefully examined and chronicled.

My life-history filled several sheets of foolscap and my examination had taken an hour and a half.

The Chief shuffled the sheets together, affixed them with a clip, then pushed them aside, sat back in his chair and, once more, glared at me without speaking. The minutes dragged past.

Would he never tell me why he had sent for me, and why he had been putting me through the Third Degree ? Hitherto I had contrived

to control both my voice and my demeanour
and to simulate a manner of polite indifference,
as though it were the most natural thing in
the world to be suddenly obliged to cancel
important engagements and to drive sixteen
kilometres, directly after breakfast, to be
questioned for two hours about my intimate
affairs, private life, and means of subsistence,
by the French police.

Suddenly the silence was broken by a
startling roar. He had spoken at last. (I will
translate the ensuing conversation.)

" You sent a telegram to Briançon, in
January, *Madame*," said the Chief of Police
in a tone of stern accusation.

I had almost forgotten, after so many weeks,
that I had sent a telegram there, but then
I remembered my message to *Mademoiselle*
and I replied, meekly—

" Yes, *Monsieur*."

He glared at me for a few moments, and
then, in the most melodramatic manner,
bending forward in his chair and glaring at
me malevolently he hissed—

" Who is Rozier ? "

I blinked at him and then, in the utmost
astonishment, replied—

" The Veterinary Surgeon of Grasse,
Monsieur."

" The Veterinary Surgeon ? " he echoed.

" Yes, *Monsieur*."

" And—who is Sophy ? "

This was fantastic ! Something began to

wobble inside me. I must not laugh. In a slightly tremulous voice I managed to reply—

"*Une chienne, Monsieur*" (I write this in French because 'lady dog' sounds ridiculous and, from mis-usage, the good old English synonym sounds, somehow, impolite).

"*UNE CHIENNE?*" positively shouted the *Chef de Police*.

"Yes, *Monsieur*," I replied and then I told him of the circumstances of that tragedy, and of my promise to *Mademoiselle*. . . .

His hand was covering his mouth under pretext of caressing that huge moustache, but I was much encouraged to notice a gleam in his eye and a slight twitching of the muscles of the face. I said nothing, but permitted myself to twinkle at him. He removed his hand, and his mouth slowly widened into a most attractive smile.

"*Une chienne!*" he repeated to himself in a whisper, and then, again, "*Une chienne!*" as he twirled his moustache. Then his body began, slightly, to shake : "*Une chienne!*" and soon we were laughing helplessly together.

When he could speak, he apologised profusely for having so deranged *Madame*. She must not be too hard on the French police if, in the observance of their duties, they had been over-zealous.

"Did you think, *Monsieur*, that Doctor Rozier and I had planned a murder?" I asked, suddenly remembering that the French never give their animals Christian names and that my innocent telegram might so have been misconstrued. But what murderer would telegraph the announcement of his crime through the Post Office? It still had not occurred to me that my message might be thought to be in code—and I, a spy.

"No, no," the *Chef* protested, "but the *Chef* of the *Sûreté* in Paris thought that your telegram was a little ambiguous and asked us to make this inquiry."

So my telegram had been sent to Paris— for the attention of the Chief of Police for all France! Hence the delay in following it up. My respect for the French secret service was greatly enhanced by this discovery.

"You have a very pretty little property, *Madame,*" bowed the *Chef*. "I came up to see you last week, but unhappily I did not find you."

If he had rung the bell and inquired for me, he might have, but (I found out later) he had not done this; he had merely spied around, doubtless to find out whether the property of the lady under suspicion was more important than her small income (well known to the Inspector of Taxes, who had all the figures) could maintain without being supplemented, perhaps, by enemy money.

Oh dear! Oh dear! OH DEAR!

With renewed apologies he bowed me out. I rushed straight to an American bar, drank a huge bowl of coffee and smoked that so-long-deferred and longed-for cigarette.

That evening I telephoned to Doctor Rozier to make an appointment for him to come and give my Dominie an injection for some puppy-ailment that was troubling him. We fixed an hour and, before saying good-night, I laughingly asked him whether he had had a visit from the police.

" The police ? " he echoed in a horror-struck voice.

Then I began to tell him the story of my visit to the *Chef*, knowing that he would enjoy the joke as much as I did—now that the matter was cleared up. The telephone, always a maddening service in France, was peculiarly exasperating that night. I was cut off no less than three times during our short conversation.

When Doctor Rozier came next day, I complained of the carelessness of the telephone operators.

" They were writing down every word you said, for the police, *Madame*," Doctor Rozier told me grimly.

This was insufferable. My line being tapped? My conversations chronicled? I assured Dr Rozier that the *Chef* had been perfectly satisfied by my explanation; had offered profuse apologies and asked me to forgive him.

"Yes," commented the old Vet., "but the trouble is that *before* your examination and explanation took place, the Post Office in Grasse must have been warned to listen-in to all your telephone conversations. You have now satisfied the Police, but they have been too busy to order the Post Office officials to relax their vigilance."

Then I remembered that, of late, the telephone girls at the Exchange had been more than usually abrupt and uncivil—even to friends who telephoned to me. The law in France, since the outbreak of hostilities, was that all telephonic conversations must be conducted in French. Many English people, my G.H.Q. Generals in particular, had floundered hopelessly in this language and had eventually had " *Parlez Francais s'il vous plait !* " barked at them continually until one of them, mad with irritation, let forth a loud " DAMN the woman," to my great refreshment. Now this access of incivility was explained.

The next day I was obliged to go down to our offices in the Carlton Hotel, Cannes, and in one of the corridors I met the Director, a charming Englishman, and could not resist sharing my Police-joke with him. He laughed immoderately for a few moments and then suddenly stopped and his face grew grave—

" No, I am not laughing any more," he said to me. " This may develop into an insufferable nuisance and haunt you until the end of the war unless it is stopped at once. The valet of a friend of mine acted foolishly and now, though all was explained satisfactorily, my friend is under suspicion and subjected to continual annoyance. You must go at once and see our British Consul in Nice, tell him all about it, and get him to put the matter into the hands of the *Préfet* of Police for the Alpes Maritimes. I do, really, urge you to do that as soon as possible."

Very much annoyed, for I was very busy, I went to Nice and saw our Consul. He, also, having enjoyed a good laugh over my story, took the same view as the Director of the Carlton. He promised to see the *Préfet* at the earliest opportunity. Two days afterwards I had a letter from the Consul saying that he had seen the *Préfet*, who was much amused by the blunder of the police, but greatly regretted the annoyance to which I had been subjected. He had informed the Gendarmerie of the Alpes Maritimes that he, personally, would vouch for my integrity and that any further inquiries must, henceforth, be addressed to him.

That night a friend happened to ring me up from Nice. The line was noisy and he is slightly deaf, so that our conversation was beset with difficulty.

"Speak *English* to the gentleman, *Madame*, he cannot understand," said the polite voice of a telephone operator from Grasse—or Nice ?——

Astonished and gratified, I obeyed.

"*Parlez Francais s'il vous plait !*" was then barked at me from the operator of Nice—or Grasse ?——

Whereupon the first voice said—

" This line has a special permit to speak
English. . . ."

So *Monsieur le Préfet* had already acted.
I poured forth a flood of my native language
down that telephone and, for the rest of the
evening, I simply purred.

This seemed to be the end of the matter,
but some weeks later I met *Mademoiselle* walking
through my olive-grove, smoking furiously and
looking extremely annoyed. In her hand flapped
a long official envelope.

" *I've* been summoned by the *Chef de Police*
of Cannes now," she said angrily. " I suppose
you've involved me in the same mess you
were in, by sending that telegram to me when
I was in a *zone reservée*. As bad luck would
have it, your wire arrived at Briançon on a
Sunday and I had gone up to Mont Genèvre
to ski, so that it followed me up there, bang
on the frontier. Now I suppose that I, too,
shall be under suspicion for the duration of
the war. I am going down to Cannes at
once."

When she returned she came up to report
to me the result of her interview. Months
before, she had gone up to our shepherd's hut,
which we had arranged as a summer holiday
place in the High Alps, to collect from it all the
blankets, mattresses, and pillows that she could
find for the use of sick soldiers. We should
never live in it again until after the war—if
ever again. From there, being near the Italian

frontier, she had sent us an ambiguous telegram, "*Toutes les cheminées fumaient*" (All the chimneys smoked). They always did, in our *bergerie*, and it was her way of letting us know that she had arrived there safely.

I was relieved to find that it was her own telegram, and not mine, which had intrigued the French police.

CHAPTER IX.

TENSION.

THE months dragged heavily by. When we were not glued to the wireless, feverishly listening to the news, we were organising golf competitions and galas to raise funds for our *Foyers des Soldats de France* and the *Entr'aide* organisation for the relief of the wives of mobilised men. I undertook the distribution of some eight hundred blankets sent by an English Society, *Amis de la France*, for the poor of the civil population. Some I delivered personally (after dark, so that the very poor, whose names I had been given, should not be humiliated by the stare of curious neighbours), and there were cases which nearly broke my heart. A woman, with eleven children lying on the floor huddled beneath a few olive sacks. Her husband had gone mad from shell-shock and was under restraint, and she had just had news that her old parents, who had lost everything in Northern France, were fleeing south to take refuge with her. Her haggard face and wild eyes haunt me still, and the way she clutched at that bundle of blankets. *" Que le bon Dieu vous bénisse, Madame,"* she croaked as she shuffled away with her load into the darkness. Thank God that she could still call upon Him, and realise that all this man-made ghastliness is not His fault.

The galas were an agony to us all; for, if we were to interest monied people in our schemes, we must put in an appearance. I hear again the heated conversations that took place among the inhabitants of our mountain before the first gala dinner.

Mademoiselle : "I'm not going. I'd rather die than go. I'm not a social person. I hate functions. You must all go and I shall go to bed."

Chorus of Neighbours: "But you'll HAVE to go. After all, the *Foyers des Soldats de France* is your baby and you'll be expected to go. And, what is more, you'll have to sit at the *table d'honneur* with the British Consul and the *Préfet* of the Alpes Maritimes."

Mademoiselle : "Nothing you can say will induce me to go. I haven't any clothes. I'd far rather give three thousand francs to the *Foyers* than spend it on a Lanvin dress that I shall never wear again." And so the discussion raged on for several nights. In the end, *Mademoiselle* consented to go if I would take a table, and, because of my illustrious military historian, represent The British Army; and if our other dear neighbour, who, when not superintending our village *foyer*, spent her time gardening or devouring every available book, would also go.

Again the question of clothes. I had only
an old Greek tea-gown of mauve and pink
chiffon, a graceful flowing affair designed by
my husband, who chose the material and the
colour-scheme, very soon after our marriage
in 1914. Being a picture-gown it did not ' date,'
but was hardly in its first youth or suitable
for a gala dinner. However, I decided that
in such a mob as we expected, no one would
notice what I wore. We all routed in our
cupboards and trunks for clothes and accessories
and I managed to find a black lace dress and
short coat for the other dear neighbour, who,
having angrily ripped off her beloved sailor's
trousers, tried on the transparent lace con-
fection and then, holding wide her draperies,
did a *pas seul* in muddy brogues, her short
men's socks and, above those, an expanse of
bare leg plainly visible. We all became quite
hysterical.

One of our Generals from G.H.Q., B.E.F.,
was on sick leave in Nice, and I was urged to
try to secure him for my table. Unfortunately
he was leaving for the Front on the very day
of the gala, but he contrived to find time to
visit John Fortescue's wife before he left. I
asked him why, when little Fort Escu contained
a spare room and John's library of military
books, had an officer of the British Army
chosen an expensive coastal hotel in which to
convalesce ? I said I knew that John would
wish his beloved British officers to be the
guests of his wife, and I begged the General

to tell this to the Commander-in-Chief when he went back. I promised to leave tired officers entirely alone to rest in the sunshine, and that I should only appear at meals to see that they were properly fed.

He told me that, until he got my message, he had no idea that I lived in this dream-place. He had had a nasty bout of influenza in the frozen-up village where G.H.Q. was then situated, and had been ordered to go south to convalesce. He had heard of Nice, because of the famous Carnivals, so he fell into a train, fell out of it at Nice and into the first hotel bus, and from there into his first hot bath for six weeks. He only regretted now that he had not known of that empty spare room in Domaine de Fort Escu ; but he would tell the C.-in-C. of my offer so that others, more fortunate than he, might profit by it.

Very soon afterwards the imminent arrival of another General and his A.D.C. was heralded by a telephone message to me from our British Consul. The C.-in-C. had taken me at my word.

I arranged the little spare room in my house for the General and the garage-flat for his Major, and when these tired men arrived I showed them their quarters. The General said to me : " I am rather jealous of Major X."

" But, General," I replied, " if you prefer the garage-flat the Major can have the spare room in Fort Escu."

" My little room is perfect," he answered.

"But you have given Major X. violets in his room. You gave me freesias, but I do love violets." Of course I rushed out to pick some for him also, while he and the Major wallowed in their hot baths. The next morning he confided to me that before going to bed he had opened his shutters and placed the bowl of violets on the table beside his bed : "So that I went to sleep with the breeze blowing the smell of those violets across my face—and I thought that I was in heaven." He asked *Mademoiselle* if he might pick one spray of mimosa from her garden, "Just so that I can say that I have actually picked a spray of mimosa in *Provence*." And the Major begged to be allowed to pick three white violets from a hedge, to send to his wife—her favourite flower. Both of them thanked me for a ' perfect ' visit when, after a very brief one, they bade me farewell.

In my heart, I thanked *them* for reminding me that, even with war shattering and maiming the world, there is peace and comfort still to be found in flowers and simple things—and people.

The last incident of that visit refreshed me more than all. The car was waiting at the door to take my soldiers to the station and the General stood in the hall, carrying his luggage, a small knapsack, and a service gas-mask (so should all great men travel in war-time).

He asked me if I thought that my *bonne* would accept from him a little present of money as a small return for her kind care of him.

" Try her, if you like, General," I said. " But I am perfectly certain that she won't accept it," and I tactfully vanished for a space. When I reappeared he was smiling ruefully. " You were right. She wouldn't hear of it. Said that *Madame* paid her well and that it was her pleasure and privilege to look after *Madame's* guests. What I wanted to give her then was a good hearty kiss."

" That," I said, " I'm sure she would have been proud to accept."

As the weeks dragged on, the fate of my devoted maid (Italian born) should Italy, after all, declare war against France, weighed almost as heavily upon my heart as I knew it did on hers. So many of her family were married in France, but her old parents lived in Piedmont, just over the frontier. Indeed Piedmont is almost as full of French as the French Riviera is full of Italians. They are all brothers and sisters. It was unbelievable, my *bonne* asserted vehemently, that such a thing as war between France and Italy could happen. If Mussolini ordained it, the Italians would not march. Yet, as she listened to the news from Rome on the wireless, the expression of her eyes became daily more distraught and I decided to drive into Nice and find out from the *Préfet* of the Alpes Maritimes what would become of Italian women living in France in case of war. Better to know one way or the other. I visited the

Préfet and also our British Consul. They were both of the unshakable opinion that Italy would remain neutral. She knew her own interests too well to declare war. She was impoverished and weakened by the Abyssinian campaign. She could never survive a complete blockade. Mussolini would continue his policy of blackmail, and, at the end of hostilities, would claim a fat reward for having kept out of the war.

" But if Italy came in," I persisted, " would you shut up my beloved *bonne* in a concentration camp ? "

To which *Monsieur le Préfet* replied : " *Madame, si nous enfermerons toutes les femmes Italiennes ici, toute la province sera vide,*" and went on to explain that as there were 180,000 Italians in and around Nice, with a great majority of women, if they were interned the province would, indeed, be nearly empty. He assured me that only the men, aged from sixteen to fifty, would be put into a concentration camp and the women, if their loyalty were guaranteed by employers or French citizens of repute, would be allowed to remain free. This assurance that my maid would not be molested in France if her country became hostile, and the strong opinion, expressed by the two people most likely to know, that Italy would never come into the war, not only quieted my *bonne* but greatly influenced me.

Since our descent from the High Alps I had scarcely seen *Mademoiselle,* who was swept into

a maelstrom of organising work, and had her
own office and secretaries in one of Cannes'
most important hotels. My job was now purely
propaganda.

I sat in my Studio at home and wrote letters,
thanking people for subscriptions and telling
them of our work, and I wrote stories about
our *foyers* and our *poilus* to be privately circulated in America. The old comradeship of
shared pioneer work was over. Although I was
busy from morning to night, I was bitterly
lonely. I missed the daily and hourly companionship of *Mademoiselle*. The old lovely
leisure was gone, and neither of us ever had a
moment in which to tend our gardens and
our beasts and birds, together, or to take our
food and drive up into the mountains in search
of the first wild flowers. The cosy interchange
of domestic news, village gossip, and of our
thoughts and ideas, once enjoyed before a
crackling fire of olive logs in *Mademoiselle's*
old *Château* or my great rock-hewn fireplace
in little ' Sunset House ' (Fort Escu) was
over. When we met now, she was always
surrounded by a crowd of eager, chattering
women volunteers. I was shocked to see how
ill she looked. She was thin as a wisp of straw
and her shadowed eyes wild and gigantic with
strain and fatigue. Since I hardly ever saw
her, I could no longer look after her, even
a little, and her appearance when I did see
her, and the knowledge that she was killing
herself with overwork, nearly broke my heart.

That, and the news that things were not going well with the French Army in the North, kept me in a state of continual anxiety and unrest. I lost interest in solitary meals, and I slept very little—loneliness, and anxiety about everything, and everybody. I had not even the comfort of letters from home. They came more and more rarely and at ever-lengthening intervals from England.

And then I, who had lived in Provence for more than ten years and had thought myself to have become nearly three-quarters French, suddenly realised that every bit of me was English! Calais had fallen into the hands of the Germans. England was in danger. Every drop of blood within me boiled and sizzled with impatient desire to get home in time to be bombed and bombarded with England.

But how could I leave my *bonne* alone in my little house at such a time? And Dominie, my little Blackness, whose warm, loving presence by day and by night had been my one comfort during these last miserable months? I could not leave my shadow. Yet, if I braved a difficult and dangerous journey with him, he might be terrified out of his wits before the end of it. If we reached England, he would be taken from me and put into a concentration camp. How would he—or I— endure the separation enforced by that six months' quarantine? Ought I to resist this burning impulse to go home and just stay quietly where I was, doing what I could for the French ? But, with the Channel ports in German hands—and now they began to fall, one after another—all communication with England would soon be cut off for the duration of the war. Could I bear the silence ? Could I do any good work here while racked with anxiety for my family at home—my brother and his four little girls—my sister and hers ?

Dominie and I went out into the darkness of the garden. The air was heavy with the scent of a thousand great white Madonna lilies coming into bloom. Soon those dim olive groves would be flecked with dancing light, for it was late in May, and in mid-June would come the fire-flies. I crept down the stone steps to my little chapel, hewn out of the solid rock, and sank upon my knees in the darkness.

" You have got to decide for me," I insisted. " I'm too tired and too bewildered by every-thing to be able to think any more. Make my way plain before me—but You must make it very plain. If You want me to stay and work for You here, then block my path to England. If I am to go home, then make it possible for me—and Dominie."

I felt a wet nose pushed against my cheek. My little Blackness had found me.

We stole upstairs to bed, and, lying very close together, we slept.

The next morning I awoke from the first peaceful sleep I had had for months. Among my local letters—(for there were none, any more, from England)—I found one from a dog-loving friend telling me of wonderful quarantine kennels in Hertfordshire if I ever needed them—a place where the only danger was that one's dog became so attached to the kennel-man that he never wanted to come away. And later in the morning the telephone shrilled in my Studio, and, when I answered the call, the voice of my French lawyer asked me if I knew of anyone living on our mountain who would be willing to sell, with furniture, or to let her house, furnished, to a lady now living on Cap Ferrat who was nervous of the coast in case of Italian invasion.

CHAPTER X.

PARADISE — LOST.

I LET my house to that English lady from Cap Ferrat, and in thirty-six hours I had to pack and remove elsewhere all my silver, crystal, and valuable books ; for, in time of war, she would not be responsible for them. The house being so small, there was no available storage place, for the lady had great possessions, which must be housed somewhere. Her furniture she would leave in her villa in the hope of letting it, furnished, if Italy still remained quiet. I decided to hire the little flat of a French friend who lives in Grasse. Because of the war she had failed to find a tenant. She would be glad of the rent and would guard my treasures for me.

There followed the most harassing and heart-rending time. All my English friends in the neighbourhood rallied round me, helping to sort, pack, or destroy the contents of cupboards and drawers. During those last hours *Mademoiselle* hardly left my side. We made up great bales of clothes for the refugees now flooding France. Better that these clothes should be useful than risk their being eaten by moth in storage; for, once gone, it was extremely unlikely that I could return to France until the end of the war, and I did not see how it could possibly be a short war. My car '*Désirée*' I gave as a parting present to *Mademoiselle*. It could be used for ambulance work.

Mademoiselle had decided to stay in France. Though American-born, finding herself alone in the world after the war of 1914, she had remained in France, bought her, then derelict, Château, converted the inside of it into a thing of great beauty and had been naturalised French. She would stay and help France.

"But you, Pegs, can probably help much more by doing pen-propaganda in England and talking of our men and our *foyers*. In any case, being English, you are quite right to go home." I felt that, having entirely surrendered my will, I had now no say in the matter. It had been decided for me. I was far too tired and miserable to plan ahead, and I found now that, as each problem presented itself, it was immediately solved for me.

All I had to do was to pack, label keys, and make inventories in a kind of dazed dream. It did not seem to be me doing those things; leaving my beloved Provence after so many years—leaving—*Mademoiselle*. But she needed me no longer; she was not herself any more, nor had she been for months. Everyone's personality, and all the gentle lovely things of life, were submerged or swept away by the red flood of war. We had all become automatons,

strange, cold machines—or rather that was
what we were all pretending to be, because,
in reality, we were all torn and bleeding inside.
We had lost that Galahad feeling we had in
1914 when we were young. Now we were
working just as hard, but we were all tired,
horror-struck, and disillusioned, and our weariness, horror, and disillusion must be hid. I
think we dared not exchange confidences for
fear of breaking down, and so the old intimacy
had to be a thing of the lovely past. *Mademoiselle* wore her mask—or was it a vizor?—
better than I did. She still had the Joan of Arc
spirit and had dedicated herself to the French
Army. She could think of nothing else, and
even her peasants were ignored. When
Christmas came, for the first time during the
many years she has lived in our village, she
gave no gifts to anyone. Not even to the
children. All her money was spent on the
soldiers. Parcels must be sent to those who
had stayed with us. Christmas trees and
festivities be provided and organised for our
foyers in the High Alps—for the wounded men
in hospitals.

But I could not so harden my heart. I had
to provide my annual Christmas presents for
all those in the village with expectant eyes.
Every day I wished that I were less vulnerable.
My armour was always slipping off. *Mademoiselle's* very seldom slid.

It did—a little—when the moment of our
parting came, before I drove away from my

' Sunset House,' in a hired car, with Dominie hugged very close in my arms.

I have a blurred vision of a small stone house bathed in hot sunlight, and of two figures, both beloved, standing outside its great gate, silent and still like statues of grief ; my *bonne*, her bowed head bound with a scarlet handkerchief, the fingers of her left hand clasping the third finger of her right hand (I had slipped a gold ring with the Fortescue motto engraved on it upon that finger as token that, whatever happened, she still belonged to me), and the slender form of *Mademoiselle*, whose face had suddenly become all eyes, staring at me. And, so, I left them. . . .

CHAPTER XI.

HIS HUGENESS.

I HAD to drive, first, to Nice to collect my passport and visa and my permit to leave the country, and also to pick up an old English officer who, having been ill in England, had been ordered to winter in the sun. He was lord of an island in the West Indies and had intended to travel there, but owing to the war his passage had been cancelled and he was marooned in Nice.

He had been a great comfort during those last miserable months, for he had somehow sensed my loneliness, and, despite his fourscore years, he made nothing of leaping upon a motor-bus and coming to spend a day with me. Even when he moved to Monte Carlo he was undeterred by that long journey, and often I would see His Hugeness striding through the olive groves towards little Fort Escu. His keen interest in world politics was only equalled by his interest in every trivial incident and accident of my domestic life, and his comments upon all these, though sometimes acid, were shrewd, sane, witty, and always sympathetic. I loved to make him laugh; to see that great Roman head thrown back and to hear the reverberating "Ha! Ha!" roar through my house; the face, grim and at times sardonic in expression, break up into the wide happy grin of a mischievous boy. Never had woman wiser or kinder counsellor or a more patient and understanding friend; and I must have been perfectly maddening at that time, for I was in a perpetual state of miserable vacillation, could concentrate my frantic thoughts upon nothing for very long nor decide anything important. During this time I was like a very storm-tossed ship. His Hugeness supplied keel, ballast, and rudder, and, best of all, he kept the flag flying at the masthead: a British Union Jack. Later he was to blow wind into sagging sails to bear that ship safely into an English port, and to see that she arrived, after so difficult a passage, with sails trimly set and the flag still flying.

His military experience taught him to be apprehensive of what might happen in France, but, being convinced that I ought to go home, instead of hastening thither himself, he remained to urge me to make instant arrangements for departure with him: " I will wait for you until May 25th," he repeated to me constantly.

" Why May 25th ? " I asked.

" I think that should be the latest date for our departure," he insisted, never giving his reason. He has since confessed that he had no reason, only instinct.

" I think you should go home." How often

did he repeat that advice, and I, argue that I could not leave my *bonne* in an empty house in war-time; that perhaps I could be more useful if I stayed where I was; that I could not leave Dominie behind, and, if I took him with me, he must be terrified out of his wits during the journey and then be put into a concentration camp at the end of it.

"I think you should go home. I will wait for you until May 25th," he reiterated.

When I implored him not to wait on the chance that I could come, but to save himself, quickly, he flatly refused to start. He did not like the idea of John Fortescue's wife undertaking so risky a journey, alone, in war-time. If she could start "not later than May 25th," he preferred to wait, in the hope of being able to escort her.

When the Channel ports began to go, his refusal to start without me added to my feverish anxieties. I felt that if he were stranded in France, far from his family, for the duration of the war it would be my responsibility. Life in Riviera coastal hotels is costly and, in case of illness, comfortless—and he had been very ill again since he came to France. I could see that he was growing anxious when he heard the war news on the wireless, his eyes became fixed and vague, his never-ceasing flow of anecdotes was frozen; then he would run his fingers through the great thatch of silver hair as he listened, and when the voice from Paris ceased to speak he would twist his huge body round towards me, make a grimace, and then lift his eyebrows inquiringly.

In fairness to so chivalrous a friend, I knew that I must put an end to this state of things by making my own decision to go—or to stay. I could not put the responsibility of deciding such a step upon him, and I was too tired and torn to be able to make up my mind. It was then that I suddenly realised what I ought to have realised long ago—that there was really no necessity whatever to go on torturing myself. I had been put into the world for some purpose and hitherto, whenever I had asked for help or guidance in my extremity, whenever I had given up feebly struggling and just surrendered my will completely, I had been shown exactly what to do.

It was then that I crept down to my little chapel in the rocks.

And now, the decision made for me and all difficulties cleared away, as I have already told, here I was with my Dominie-pup held very close in my arms sitting beside our faithful chauffeur, Jean, whose hired car had ever been at our service for so many years, and who was the good friend of us all, driving to Nice to pick up His Hugeness.

We bumped away down the stony approach to my little Fort, made so infinitely worse since the advent of the military; past my little signpost, now knocked drunkenly on one side by an Army lorry; and the old farm-house where lived *Monsieur* and *Madame* Pagani who had sold me the picturesque ruin which is now Fort Escu (' Sunset House ') ; narrowly avoided slaying their ugly goat which jumped (attached to chain) across our path, and so (the goat having been led by Jean back to her tethering-post) on, and up, and out on to the *Route Nationale* leading to Nice.

Not once did I look back. I should have seen nothing if I had. Jean was wonderful. He never spoke nor looked at me until, at last, I could speak to him, and by that time Dominie had saved my face by licking it dry. I could not have had two more sympathetic and understanding companions, and, forty minutes later, I had a third when His Hugeness, wearing a very spick-and-span travelling suit of light grey and a triumphant grin, levered his great body into the car.

Because of his bulk and the length of his legs, I ordained that he should pack himself with a very odd assortment of hand-luggage into the back of the car while I continued to sit next to Jean.

We drove first to the *Gendarmerie* where I was to pick up my *Permis de Voyager*, and, giving Dominie to His Hugeness, I laboured up the interminable stone stairs, almost having to fight my way through the mob of refugees and would-be travellers which crowded every floor. But thanks to the wonderful *laisser passer* given to me and to *Mademoiselle* in recognition of our work for the French Army, I found all my papers ready and waiting for me in the hands of courteous, smiling French officials. They had given me a permit to return to France, because, they said, it was inconceivable that I should not come back.

My English lawyer and his wife in Nice had made out for me a route to the coast by devious little-known byways. They had followed it themselves one summer when on holiday.

" If you follow this route you are much less likely to get held up for papers and formalities. Speed is very necessary if you are to get out of France now. Calais has gone—Boulogne has gone—probably le Havre and Cherbourg will be closed by the time you get to the coast. I should make for Brittany and try St Nazaire," advised my man of law. " You will find the main roads choked with refugees from Belgium and Northern France."

The first two hours of that journey had to be borne—somehow. We had to turn round again, but this time we took the coast road, passing through loved and familiar places : Cagnes, that little ancient town perched on its hill ; old, fortified Antibes dreaming beside the blue sunlit sea ; dear Cannes, her loyal subjects stolen from her by war, still bravely striving to keep her place as the gay Queen of the Riviera coastal towns. We drove down the Croisette, deserted save by a few white-clad manicurists hurrying from *Antoine's* to their *déjeûner*. There were some depressed people drinking their *aperatifs* beneath the striped

linen umbrellas on the terrace of the Hotel
Carlton. I looked up at the windows of our
offices where *Mademoiselle* would doubtless still
toil on amid a noisy crowd, organising more
and still more of her *Foyers des Soldats de
France;* she, who so hated towns and their
life, who was only happy when among mountains,
flowers, birds, and beasts—*Mademoiselle !* . . .

Those blank windows released the dam I
had been trying to build against the flood of
happy, happy memories which nearly drowned
me now. Camping with *Mademoiselle* under
the snows of the High Alps ; in valleys starred
with narcissi and Paradise lilies ; grilling fish
upon a charcoal brazier under the vine pergola
outside our tiny cottage built upon the rocks
beyond St Tropez. Afterwards, watching fisher-
men, with flares, harpooning fish from little
black boats on a moonlit sea, seen through
the great spears of agaves, black against the
silver radiance. *Mademoiselle*, the ideal companion of the old days which now seemed so
far distant, a slim trousered figure cooking
delicacies for our supper in our little *bergerie*
opposite the Meije glacier ; the crooning of
negro spirituals heard upon the shore of our
lovely bay before the Douaneries, below
Ramatuelle, while we bathed, at night, in a
phosphorescent sea ; *Mademoiselle* drawing my
portrait as I wrote in the lovely little inn of
St Virgilio on Lake Garda when we toured
Italy in my '*Désirée*' ; memories of *Mademoiselle* with our dogs—almost a dog herself

in her understanding of their needs, their ailments, and, I verily believe, their thoughts ; *Mademoiselle*—a war-time *Mademoiselle*, transformed into a thin, white-faced ghost with haunted eyes, hard and silent, save when she was with her *poilus* in her *Infirmerie*, when she became an angel of gentleness and mercy, treating them tenderly as though they were children of her blood. . . .

" Jean," I burst out suddenly to the silent man by my side, nursing the engine of his great car with such proud skill as we climbed the Esterels, " have you ever felt so much inside that it became a physical pain ? " A queer question to ask a chauffeur, but Jean—was Jean—and a Frenchman. He shot a swift glance of very blue eyes, and his dark saturnine face was suddenly illumined with a wonderful smile of sympathy and understanding—

" *Mais oui, Madame,*" he answered simply.

" It will be better, Jean," I said, " when we reach strange country."

He pressed the accelerator and the car rushed ahead, past the familiar turning to St Tropez, and then turned inland. Loved landmarks were left behind.

CHAPTER XII.

DISCIPLINING DOMINIE.

WE had been warned that ours would be a
difficult, perhaps a dangerous journey and
that we might not be able to get out of France
at the end of it. This was one of the reasons
that I had begged Jean to take me in his car,
for, at worst, we could go back with him to
the Midi. For the rest, once we had left that
beloved part of the country, I felt a strange
feeling of elation as the fighting spirit of
adventure began to rise, slowly, in my veins
like sap of trees in spring. And if we believe
in personal guardian angels, it is reasonable,
also, to believe that God, the Divine Organiser,
must put those in charge of us who knew and
loved us best on earth. So that when Jean
stopped at intervals to consult his Michelin
map, I restrained the zeal of His Hugeness
who, like all soldiers, had always better ideas
than civilians and wanted to stage-manage
our journey, because I knew that John Fortescue,
that Master of Maps, was quietly guiding Jean
for all our good. When we reached some
common land ablaze with gorse and golden
broom, I felt Daddie very near—he loved all

golden flowers—and it was he, I felt, who prompted Jean to ask the way of a simple peasant sitting on a heap of stones. I could almost hear Daddie's delighted laugh when the man directed us to the *patte de poule* two kilometres ahead—a place where roads met, not in the form of a cross but of a hen's foot Ψ. And it was Mummie, I know, who put it into my head to buy provisions very early in the day lest, farther along the road, we found that locust-refugees had eaten up everything. I thought of this just as we were passing a hedge of wild roses. Daddie always said that Mummie was just like them, wilful in her growing, sweet and lovely, but withal prickly on occasion, strong and wild, but liking the support of some strong and sheltering hedge (himself).

Our road was very beautiful, winding through woods and crossing great rivers. Tiring, though, for Jean as driver. I made Dominie the excuse for several halts, when I wandered with him awhile in cool copses and we both bathed our faces in water springing from the crevices of fern-clad rocks while Jean and His Hugeness soaked their handkerchiefs to mop hot faces, then smoked cigarettes by the side of the car.

Very early on our journey we began to meet Belgian refugees rushing southwards, their cars stacked with luggage of every description. I remarked to Jean that every car had a mattress on its roof and that these people were prudent to carry their sleeping accommodation with them, since they might find none in hotels and inns. Jean smiled grimly as he told me that the mattresses were placed as some little protection against the machine-gunning of pursuing German aeroplanes.

Soon the occasional Belgian cars passed us more frequently, until at last they followed each other so quickly that they formed one long procession. If so many Belgians had sought and found our tortuous route leading to the Midi, what must the conditions of the main roads be like to-day? I blessed my lawyer. Jean was obliged to use his klaxon at every bend of the road, and my nervous Dominie grew more and more restless. Sharp noises send him frantic. He climbed up my arm and craned his neck as far out of the window as possible, placing one floppy front paw on its edge and the other on my head while his back toes clawed the flesh of my knees in his effort to balance. He changed his position every moment and all my endeavours to make him settle down quietly failed. He was making me very hot and weary, when suddenly I heard an insistent knocking on the pane of the glass partition behind me, and turned, to find that His Hugeness had heaved his great frame forward and was trying to make me hear something. I slid back the glass panel.

" Give him to me," he said quietly.

" But he hardly knows you," I objected. " He is the most self-willed dog I ever met. If he wants to look out of the window he will look out of the window, and he'll trample on your face to get there. He's scared. He'll send you quite mad with his fidgeting."

"No, he won't. Give him to me," commanded H.H., and forthwith seized my trembling little Blackness and hauled him through the aperture into the back of the car. Dominie did not know whether to be more frightened or furious. He sat, panting, by the side of H.H., restrained from active protest by one great hand on his collar, rolling indignant and apprehensive glances sideways at the giant by his side, and then frantic appeals to me, trembling convulsively as he sat.

"I had rather have him here. He wasn't really worrying me much," I faltered weakly.

"He was tiring you out. He is very well here. Better for you and better for him. It is cooler here and, with the partition shut, he will hear that klaxon less."

For the next hour I could not resist casting furtive glances behind me, and always they were met by a little nod and a reassuring smile from H.H. At first he held Dominie firmly by the collar. Soon he sat on the end of my puppy's lead so that his hand might be free to caress the silky head and ears. After a time Dominie began to blink. At last he was growing sleepy. To my amazement he, always so terrified of all men save Jean, laid his head upon H.H.'s knee and closed his eyes. H.H. began to nod, but still his hand drowsily caressed the little dog's head. The next time I looked round both of them were peacefully asleep.

The disciplining of Dominie began that day, but it was with satisfaction I noticed that, even in the care of a large man who would stand no nonsense, my indomitable span'l managed to get round him now and then. His Hugeness was gradually and unconsciously succumbing to his charm. Although, when we halted for refreshment in little towns and villages, Dominie was being trained not to fight like a tiger to get out of the car first, nearly strangling himself with his lead and overbalancing his leader—although, the first time this happened to His Hugeness, I heard a quiet but very firm voice say : " No. *I* get out first," and saw Dominie's face of sheer amazement as a huge hand was put forth completely blocking his passage ; it was from that same hand that the first hunk of *buttered* tea-cake was given to my dog.

CHAPTER XIII.

LOSS AND LUCK.

REFRESHED by our short intervals of rest, Jean always made up for lost time by speeding ahead afterwards. As we were the only car going north this was possible. (We grew accustomed to the astonished stare of peasants, loitering outside their cottages to watch the stream of Belgian cars rushing south. Who could these madmen be, going north—into hell?) As we were racing along, I was suddenly startled by a flying object which whizzed past the window and fell with a thud on the road. As it did not explode it could not be a bomb. There was a stifled execration from Jean as he applied his brakes and we slid to a standstill in a cloud of dust.

" What *has* happened ? " I asked.

" *Le bagage!* " moaned Jean. " *J'avais raison. Ah! mon Dieu!* "

It was indeed our luggage—a duffle bag of mine and a suitcase of H.H. had slipped their moorings on the roof and now lay in a ditch— luckily a dry ditch—and unburst. I began counting the remaining packages to reassure Jean, but he turned piteous eyes on me and

whispered the tragic news that the *second* suitcase of *Monsieur le Commandant* was nowhere
to be seen. It must have slipped off the back
of the roof and—where was it now? What
hope of ever retrieving it when literally thousands of Belgian cars, filled with refugees who
would be so thankful for such a find, had
passed us all day long?

His Hugeness bore the blow with fortitude,
although (of course) it was the suitcase containing his shirts and collars and, most tragic
of all, his decorations—all his miniature medals
—a long line of them.

Jean had parked the car at the side of the
road and locked it up, so we all turned back
on foot, retracing our steps and searching the
ditches and hedges on either side of the road—
in vain.

I persuaded H.H. to let Jean drive us back
to the last village we had passed and there
to leave all details of his loss and his destination
with the Mayor. H.H. thought it was but a
waste of time—and we had no time to waste—
but he yielded to entreaty and did as we
suggested. He spent a hot and weary half-
hour in the crowded parlour of the Mayor's
private house where the poor man was struggling
with the awful problem of how, and where,
to house and feed some hundreds of poor
Belgian refugees with whom his house and the
entire village were packed. He was polite,
if, excusably, *distrait*. No suitcase had been
brought to him as yet, but if one were, he

would send it on to the next town. H.H.
emerged shaking his head sorrowfully and,
with a little grimace of resignation, heaved
himself into the car. Dominie, sensing his
depression, with an apologetic look at me
climbed on to his knees and laid his head on
the great shoulder.

For the next few miles, I cast anxious glances
at the two over mine, and once, as we passed
through a small town, I saw the eyes of His
Hugeness gazing mournfully at the advertisement *CHEMISERIE* over a shop and knew
that he was reflecting that no ready-made shirt
would ever fit his enormous frame. He must
suffer the misery of wearing the same shirt
and collar, in this heat—indefinitely. Poor
H.H.! What a reward for chivalry.

Until now we had had no difficulty in securing
three good rooms in the best hotel at the end of
our long and tiring days, but we were approaching a zone which would certainly be crowded
with refugees both rich and poor. It was very
doubtful if we should find a lodging in the next
town, Villefranche (on the border of the provinces
of Tarn and Lot), still many kilometres away,
and the misfortune of the suitcase had delayed
us until dusk was falling. It was nearly dark
when we arrived there, to find it packed with
people, and cars parked in every available
space. Feeling fairly certain of the reply we
should get everywhere, we nevertheless inquired
for rooms in one or two hotels. As we had
anticipated, the answer was always the same,

not a vacant room to be had in the town. Jean looked grey with fatigue; he had had a tiring and twisty drive in the heat during many hours and the disaster of the luggage had finished him. It would be sheer cruelty to suggest that we adventure farther, and probably we should find the same congestion everywhere. I decided to play the first of my two trump cards, held hitherto in reserve. I would seek out the head of the *Gendarmerie*, show him my membership card of the *Amicale de la Police* of the Alpes Maritimes to which I had belonged since my husband and I first came to live in Provence in 1931, and enlist his aid. Accordingly I asked Jean to drive to the little *Place*, a lovely square surrounded by ancient tiled houses with crazy gables and quaint little turrets silhouetted against the afterglow in the evening sky. It was filled with cars and carts and noisy gesticulating Belgians who, having failed to find sleeping accommodation in the town, were discussing the idea of taking their mattresses from the roofs of their cars and stretching them out upon the pavement.

Standing before the door of the *Gendarmerie* were a group of policemen talking together. I addressed a striped one and, after producing my *Amicale* card, asked for his advice and help. He made a gesture which encircled the already overcrowded Square, then shrugged his shoulders saying: "*Je regrette Madame. Il-n'y-a absolument rien.*"

I refused to believe that there was absolutely

nothing left by way of sleeping accommodation in the town, and then I pointed upwards to a delicious little turreted tower in a corner and told the police that I should love to sleep up there. They laughed and told me that it had long been abandoned as an habitation— it had no windows, no furniture, no bedding.

" But I have here blankets and cushions, my camp equipment," I assured them. " At least we should have a roof over our heads, privacy, and, surely, a glorious view in the morning."

The idea seemed to tickle them enormously, but it did more, it suggested another to the Sergeant. If *Madame* really meant what she said and could be content with lodging as humble as that, he thought perhaps that he might be able to find some simple shelter for us all, less primitive than the *tourelle*. He strode off and vanished down one of the many side streets, leaving us in conversation with his subordinates.

Suddenly a telephone bell shrilled from somewhere inside the building and after a few moments the head of a *gendarme* poked out of an upper window—

" Has any gentleman here lost a suitcase ? " he bawled in French. " The Mayor of X. is on the telephone and he tells me . . ." He was interrupted by a joyful roar from H.H., and there followed an indescribably animated and noisy duologue, the *gendarme* yelling particulars of the name, address, and labels upon the suitcase, and H.H. bellowing assurances that it was his and proofs of ownership. Then the head at the upper window vanished inside while its owner made arrangements with the Mayor of X. for the transfer of the errant suitcase to Villefranche, and H.H. wheeled upon me with the most ecstatic grin I ever saw and the little Square rocked and reverberated with his triumphant "Ha, ha!" What luck! What marvellous, incredible luck that the suitcase should have been picked up by a fleeing Belgian car and deposited at the very village where H.H. had reported its loss! Jean was speechless and almost tearful with happiness and relief. His smile was just as ecstatic as that of H.H. Mine must have been fairly wide, and it widened still further when our Sergeant of Police reappeared, smiling broadly too, to inform us that he had found lodging for us with a friend who kept a small eating-place. " *Très, très simple*," he apologised, but at least it was clean and its owners *braves gens*. There was a fairly large room containing two good beds for *Monsieur* and *Madame*, and there was an alcove in the landing passage—it had no window, but it had a door, and a mattress could be put there for the chauffeur.

My smile froze as he spoke and his eyes expressed hurt surprise when the rapturous exclamations he had expected from me were never uttered. I thanked him very warmly for all his trouble, but insisted that we must

have three bedrooms. He was beginning to
protest when I drew him aside and quickly
explained in an undertone that the gentleman
travelling with us was not my husband but a
chivalrous English officer who would not allow
me to attempt a journey to England, in war-
time, without the protection of a male. Therefore we must have three bedrooms, one for me,
one for *Monsieur le Commandant*, and one for
the chauffeur. The Sergeant shrugged his
shoulders, looked at me with a gentle reproving
smile and murmured: " *Madame! Il ne faut
pas être trop exigeante en temps de guerre.*"

I solved the problem by suggesting to H.H.
that he should share the big room with Jean,
who, having done all the work that day, had
need of a good night's rest in a comfortable
bed ; while Dominie and I shared the ' alcove '
on the landing—which proved to be nothing
more than a spacious cupboard. H.H. never
saw it or he would have made a scene, and
poor Jean was in an agony to think of *Madame*
sleeping on a straw mattress in that black hole.
However, my little Dominie curled up under
my knees and we spent a happy, if extremely
uncomfortable night together in our cupboard.
It was hot and airless, for the door must be
kept shut, as it opened on to the landing along
which soldiers and refugees constantly passed
at all hours during that long night on their
way to bed, and the straw pricked through the
mattress, but at least the Blackness and I were
together, under shelter, and could lie down. I

had had visions of all four of us crouched in cramped attitudes in the car, parked in some public place amid a swarm of unwashen refugees. We should now be able to wash ourselves and be served with hot coffee in the morning. I blessed that kind *gendarme*, and, if he had known the sequel of his intervention, I do not think he could any longer have scolded me for being *exigeante*, he would only have thought me completely mad to prefer a straw mattress in a cupboard to a comfortable bed.

CHAPTER XIV.

TRAGIC BELGIUM.

THE next day was one of delays and exasperation. We had reached a difficult stage of our journey, and to get to St Nazaire, the port for which we were making, we must necessarily travel for a time along main roads and pass through important towns now congested with Belgians. Here the car must crawl in first or second gear, with Jean hooting warnings every few moments until the nerves of all of us, especially those of Dominie, were frayed.

When we got out to search for some place in which to eat our *déjeûner* he was trembling in every limb and slavering with heat and terror. The climax came when a great electric tram, the first he had ever seen, screamed round the corner and thundered towards us. I had him firmly on a shortened lead, but when he saw this Horrible Monster apparently about to fall upon him he cast one wild and agonised look around, saw His Hugeness crossing the street ahead of him and, with a desperate strength, made for him, towing me behind, regardless of impeding pedestrians whom we bumped, tripped up and nearly overturned, until he reached that mass of protective flesh that had proved his solace and defence throughout the journey. Only a man as big as that could save a little Cocker in this moment of terror.

And H.H. understood. With one great hand he swept up my little Blackness under his arm murmuring consolatory phrases and, together, they crossed that seething thoroughfare. Later, seated between the legs of H.H. in a crowded restaurant, he was induced to eat succulent morsels of *filet de bœuf*, and that awful trembling ceased.

Never once during that trying journey did the big man lose patience with the little dog, nor with me, and I wonder which of us tried it most.

I have not spoken of the time we lost in making inquiries in every town we visited and in telephoning to various officials in towns ahead of us, always trying to find out which ports were still open to English ships and never receiving any satisfactory information. But always we had been advised to make for St Nazaire and we were nosing our way thither.

Tulle—Limoges—Poitiers, and here the press of people was so great that it was hardly possible to enter the town. Progress had become increasingly painful as we travelled northward, meeting, now, the tragic host of Belgian poor, fleeing on foot with their shapeless bundles ; mothers carrying tiny babies and dragging small white-faced children by the hand, old people crawling along supported by the young, others pushing perambulators, hand-carts, or ancient bicycles piled with pathetic household goods. Already the kind French were adopting these poor refugees, and in every village we met fussy cheerful French officials shepherding crowds of them to the Mairie where accommodation would be allotted and food given to them. Every village street was double-lined with stationary cars of every description, many of them making their last halt, for the petrol pumps were dry. I peeped into one tiny closed car while Jean was making a futile inquiry for *essence* at a garage, and saw five small children, clustered on cushions, fast asleep. They looked so pretty, relaxed in the lovely abandon of youth ; arms thrown above heads or stretched across another plump little body, legs flung out anyhow, but the posture always graceful, dark heads touching blonde heads. *Leonardo da Vinci* would have loved to draw them. Seated on the running-board of the car, a very small baby in her arms, was a young woman, bare-headed, her golden hair blown in wisps about her face, talking, as I came up, to a French workman who had brought her some water in a tin cup to mix with milk for her baby. I asked her if the bouquet of flowers within the tiny car was hers. She nodded, smiling. Yes, they were her children. They had all travelled for many days and nights from Belgium. She had lost house, furniture, money, everything, " But," she said triumphantly, "what does that matter? I have my treasure safely here, my husband and my children," and she beamed happily at a man who came hurrying up to tell her that there was no more petrol to be had in the village. They looked at each other and laughed. She raised her eyebrows, shrugged her shoulders, and began placidly to feed her baby. What did anything matter now? They were safely in France.

In Poitiers the confusion was indescribable. We were told that the Belgian Government had just arrived and had taken up their quarters in the hotel where H.H. had hoped to have luncheon. From Poitiers they would continue to administer Belgian affairs and prosecute the conduct of the war. News of their arrival had flown around the neighbourhood, and Belgians, civilians and soldiers, thenceforth all directed their cars and footsteps towards Poitiers, certain that where their Government was, there also would be their King. There were so many gorgeous uniforms and gold-braided officials in Poitiers that we, too, were convinced that King Leopold and his Court had arrived, and I told Jean to get out of the town as quickly as he could to seek lodging somewhere in the country before night fell.

Jean was completely bewildered. So great was the throng of people in the streets and the congestion of traffic that he could only go with the stream, for, if he stopped for a moment, yells of execration and the scream of

a hundred protesting klaxons rent the air.
Chance gave him at last an opportunity to turn
into a side-street which led down to the main
railway station, but here confusion was worse
confounded for a train had just come in and
was belching forth Belgians in hundreds. These
streamed forth from the station yard and fought
their way into the already crowded Square.
A Belgian policeman had been put on as an
' extra ' to regulate the traffic at this point.

Jean gradually edged his car in the direction
of the white tin-hat worn by the Belgian police,
conspicuous above the surging mass of human
beings. When we had approached within shouting distance Jean asked him the way to Mirebeau.
The policeman gave him one frenzied look,
threw his arms heavenward in a despairing
gesture, and cried almost tearfully : " *Monsieur,
je suis ici il-y-a dix minutes !* "

How could he be expected to direct anyone,
anywhere, when he had himself only arrived
in Poitiers ten minutes ago ? So we found
our own way out of Poitiers.

To our great surprise we discovered a humble
hotel in Mirebeau with three empty bedrooms,
small but clean, floored with well-scrubbed
boards ; a tin wash-stand, a chair, and a bed
formed the furnishing of each. In ours, Dominie
and I slept the sleep of the totally exhausted.

We were awakened by shouting voices in
the street next morning. I peered out of the
window and saw a crowd of gesticulating men
engaged in violent altercation which looked

as though it might end in a free fight, fists
clenched, purple faces thrust forward, and
all the rest of it. An unusual scene for France
in the early morning when citizens are usually
lapping up sopped bread soaked in bowls of
café-au-lait and reading their morning papers
in amity. What could so have disturbed them?
I was soon to learn. When Dominie towed
me dangerously down the staircase, intent
upon making more enemies of vulgar dogs
in the Square, I found H.H. seated by an iron
table on the terrace outside, glowering gloomily
at space. When he became aware of our presence,
announced by the possessive paw of Dominie
batting his thigh, he rose heavily to his feet.

"Leopold * has let us down," he whispered
hoarsely.

"Leopold?" I echoed stupidly, still only
half-awake.

"Leopold of Belgium. The Belgian Prime
Minister has announced it this morning. God
only knows what will happen now. Our army
is fairly trapped."

We stared at each other silently.

"I *won't* believe it," I said at length.

"It is all too true," groaned H.H. "The
Belgian Prime Minister announced it on the
wireless—and then——! Didn't you hear the
row going on down here? Belgians who, like
you, refused to believe it, and Frenchmen
frantic because, through Belgian treachery, their

* At this moment of world-wide shock and horror no one knew
of the tragic frustration of the Belgian King's efforts to warn
England and France of the predicament of his overwhelmed army.

relatives who have gone North to help Belgium will now, together with the English, be trapped and almost certainly cut to pieces by the Germans. One young Belgian cried out : ' *Vive le Roi !* ' Frenchmen set upon him—and the police did not intervene. . . . Are you packed up ? We had better get on at once. I very much doubt if we can get out of France now. Every available boat will be needed to get our men off—IF they can get to the coast. Good God, what a mess ! "

" If you will find Jean and tell him to get the luggage down, I will just take Dominie for a run and then we'll start," I said quietly.

John's army ! His beloved army ! Oh—if their retreat to the sea was cut off——

The horror of that thought turned me sick. . . .

Our personal plight mattered nothing in the face of that great tragedy.

A grave-faced Jean was already seated before the wheel when Dominie and I completed our tour of the Square. How glad I was that I had hired a car and secured Jean's personal service. If all the ports were closed to us, we could, at worst, return with him to the Midi, there to remain for the duration of the war—which might last all our lives. I bundled a protesting Dominie into the back of the car with his Big Protector and climbed in myself beside Jean.

" *Il faut aller vite, Jean,*" I said to him.

" *Je crois bien, Madame,*" he answered grimly.

And after that we did go, very quickly.

147

CHAPTER XV.

WE TRAVERSE BRITTANY.

LIVING in the Midi, enjoying always its contrast
of dazzling colour with soft silver grey and black ;
the hot incredible blue of sky and sea and the
mad profusion of vivid flowers, seen amid dim
olive groves stabbed through by dark cypresses
—I had not believed that anything lovelier
could exist in France. Yet, as we left all this
behind and wound our way westward through
great forests bordered by wide glittering rivers,
which dwindled sometimes into noisy torrents
obstructed by great rocks ; as we passed through
ancient little towns, and villages of houses
with roofs and crazy gables that would have
delighted Durer's eyes ; saw ancient farms
with lovely turreted pigeon-houses, and old
stained tiles or slated roofs sloped at odd angles ;
came upon massive ruined fortresses perched
high upon rock-cliffs, and twin-towered gate-
ways leading into walled towns ; I was amazed
by the beauty and the infinite variety of this
country I was leaving. And suddenly we were
winding through vivid green pasture-land
through which babbled little streams fringed
with willow-herb ; honeysuckle clambered over

hedges and we passed through the green gloom of beech and oak and chestnut woods. But this might be England! The thought flashed into my mind that perhaps we were being given, here in France, one glimpse of the loveliness that is ours in England in May—because we might never see it again in our own country.

I turned to His Hugeness who was gazing drowsily out of the window nursing an upside-down Dominie in both arms like a sleeping baby, and called to him—

"Even if we die in France, we have seen England again!"

He nodded and smiled softly at the scenery without, then turned his eyes on me, and I saw that they were wet.

As we sped onwards towards the coast of Brittany, the woods on either side of the road thinned and gradually slipped back into the distance. Clumps of willows replaced them, and hedges tangled with wild roses bordered flat fields in which grazed peaceful cows. Next came common-land patched with flowering gorse, and gradually the vegetation grew sparser, the ground was humped at intervals by granite rocks standing amid coarse tufts of rush-like grass, and then, stark and solitary against a misty sky, a wayside Calvary, symbol of sacrifice and suffering.

I thought of the words of one, much-beloved, who had said to me in parting: "God bless you and keep you safe. Every day I will send this message to you, even though the world is being crucified."

The world *was* being crucified and, thinking of John's soldiers in their peril; of my beloved France and the lovely little home that I had left, perhaps for ever; of—*Mademoiselle*—I, too, felt the piercing of nails and thorns and spear and, unable to bear the pain alone, I shared it with that lonely Figure, that tortured but triumphant Christ. . . .

I slid back the glass panel behind me and signed to H.H. to give me my Blackness, who did not wait to be lifted but kicked and scrambled himself through the aperture on to my shoulder, greeting me as though I had just returned from the North Pole. . . . There is such comfort in the love and companionship of dogs. Only a God of love—and humour—could have thought of creating such faithful funny things for the happiness of His children. . . .

I remember St Nazaire as the emptiest place I have ever seen. The grey misty sea was completely empty of ships, the wide endless promenade above it was equally empty of people. Not even a dog was in sight. After fighting one's way through the noisy over-crowded streets of inland towns this stillness was startling, and the loneliness of it almost uncanny.

We wanted to find the Port officials, but there was nobody of whom to inquire. We told Jean to drive slowly before the endless row of buildings facing the shrouded sea.

Depression clouded my spirit as we passed
these dreary houses in review, tall and pale,
like spectres, with sad blank windows like
mourning eyes staring out over that empty sea.

The sea could not have been emptier, not
even a little fishing-boat in sight. And, slowly,
I realised the cause of my depression. Had
English boats still been visiting this port the
town would have been packed with refugees.
I looked over my shoulder at H.H. who was
regarding the passing brass plates and painted
boards on the gates and doors of those houses
with eyes heavy with gloom ; all were dead,
and empty.

Was he wondering, as I was, whether we were
to be stranded in this desolate place for weeks,
or months, waiting for a boat that perhaps
would never come ?

Dominie grew restive. When the pace of
the car slowed down, this generally meant
that it would presently stop and that Jean
would open the door. Liberty ! Lamp-posts !
I suggested to Jean that we might continue
this search for the British Consulate or the
offices of the Harbour - master on foot, and
while the Blackness towed me from pillar
to post along that endless promenade, Jean
and H.H. continued to study brass door-plates.

A shout from the latter told me that he had
found what he sought, and I saw his huge
frame disappear through a doorway. He reappeared after a few moments and beckoned
to me. He had discovered a Naval Commander

inside the building whose distant cousin had
married an even more distant cousin of his.
Marvellous coincidence! H.H. was beaming
and was soon launched on a tide of reminiscences
and anecdotes which did not promise to carry
us towards the harbour where we would be.
I ventured to cut in with a timid inquiry as
to our chances of an English boat.

. The Commander shook his head. " Nothing
is going out or coming in here," he said, " and,
I imagine, no chance of a boat in the future."

Evidently pitying my blank expression of
dismay, he added, " We know nothing here.
But the British Consul at Nantes tells us to
advise anyone looking for an open port to try
St Malo."

I felt better. But then he dunched me again.
" Of course it may be closed by the time you
get there. The Bosche is sweeping down the
coast pretty swiftly now."

Well, then, we must lose no more time, and
poor tired Jean must take the wheel again and
drive like the devil.

We were warned that our progress would be
impeded every few yards if we took the coast
route. At every cross-roads our papers and
passports would be examined and Jean would
have to slow down constantly to wriggle the
car through S and Z shaped barricades of
concrete blocks. We had already passed through
several barriers on the inland route as we
approached the coast, peasant-made obstructions
of piled logs, empty petrol drums, tangled barbed

wire, old wheel-barrows, and once a derelict steam-roller lying on its side, and these had delayed us.

We were not anxious for multiplication of these obstructions and so we left that bleak desolation that was St Nazaire and once again turned inland.

Jean looked grey with fatigue, and, not for the first time during those exhausting days, I filled the cup of my little pocket flask with brandy and handed it to him. With a quick look of gratitude he took it with one hand and drained it without slackening speed.

" *Courage, mon brave Jean*," I whispered, for we had nearly reached our journey's end. Redon passed, Rennes behind us, soon we should be in St Malo.

We drove into St Malo at sunset. The tide had gone out, leaving a vast expanse of shining wet sand jewelled with sea-pools reflecting the flaming colours of the sky. The fortified walls and towers of the old town were silhouetted black against this flaming glory. How familiar was this place! I remembered the lovely holidays spent in Brittany during my married life and the thrill our arrival in St Malo always gave me. The thrill was there now—but different—more poignant, very apprehensive.

We drove to the Hotel de l'Univers with not much hope of finding rooms, but, to our astonishment and infinite relief, we were given a choice of them. My brain, at the moment, could only think of two things—beds and baths for us all, and until I heard H.H. expressing his astonishment to the Manager at the emptiness of the hotel, the reason for this phenomenon had not occurred to me. The Manager's reply was therefore something of a shock—

" *The boat for England left an hour ago, Monsieur.* If you had arrived yesterday morning I could not even have given you space for a rug on the floor. The town was crowded out with refugees—English, Belgian, and French from Paris, Calais, Boulogne, Le Havre, Cherbourg, and the northern provinces. There were trains drawn up in sidings at the station packed with English who were obliged to live in their railway carriages for three days. You have just arrived at a lucky moment, for, in half an hour, more trains are due and it will be the same thing—or worse—all over again."

H.H. tilted his hat back and gave a long whistle of dismay.

" The boat has gone," he repeated softly, then looked at me, grimaced and shrugged his shoulders. Still, I could only think of two things, BATH and BED. Once washed and rested, I felt that I could bear anything.

One more duty lay before me and then I could enjoy them. The Blackness must have his dinner and his final run. I was told that all dogs must be fed in the scullery, and I was shown a steamy noisy place where scullions and waiters jostled each other amid a stench of cooking food. I knew that Dominie would never touch anything in such a place and that I should die in it. Therefore, with my last spark of energy, I asked the favour of a talk with the chef, and, when he presently appeared in his tall white cap, I explained the situation, rather piteously I expect, and begged him to send up a piece of grilled meat and some plainly cooked vegetables which my nervous little dog might eat in my tiled bathroom. I swore that he should soil no carpet. The chef consented and, as I shook hands with him, I pressed into one palm a *pourboire*. Then Dominie and I climbed up to the fourth floor.

I liked my big bedroom at once. It smelt of the past, had a great wide bed with a ruby velvet coverlet and heavy curtains of the same material shrouding the windows. It was old-fashioned, but looked, somehow, welcoming and safe. The white-tiled bathroom was clean and modern. Dominie also liked the room. Soon afterwards a knock on the door heralded the arrival of his supper, which was brought in by a smart waiter bearing a shining tray on which reposed a white metal plate with a piece of grilled meat and no less than three bowls, containing carrots, spinach, and spaghetti. The chef had rather exaggerated the favour I had asked, but my Blackness did deserve a banquet after such a long and, to him, terrifying journey.

Afterwards we prowled around inside the fortified walls, finding an inner square with a plot of grass in the centre, and, as we were returning to the hotel, a voice called to me,

" *Cigarette Anglaise, Mademoiselle ?* " The words
were French, but the accent very English,
and the voice came from the driver's seat of
a stationary car and it belonged to an English
private soldier ! I very nearly kissed him,
and, with joy, accepted my first English
cigarette. My silver curls may have dis-
appointed him, but he was evidently feeling
as lonely as I was and glad to gossip even with
a *Madame*. He told me that he was chauffeur
to an officer of the English Military Police
who was ' spy-huntin' ' at that moment. " Fifth
column. Town full of 'em. You'll 'ear shots
all night. Jerry's comin' nearer every hour
and 'e always begins 'is campaigns like this,"
he reassured me. " Stayin' at that 'otel ? "
he indicated the Hotel de l'Univers with a jerk
of the thumb. " Ground floor back, I 'ope ?
We're expectin' planes. This is the last port
to go."

" I'm on the fourth floor front," I told him,
" and the whole German Army won't do me
out of my hot bath or keep me out of my bed
to-night." And they did not. Dominie and
I fell asleep lulled by the shouts, shots, and
screaming whistles of the English military police.

CHAPTER XVI.

SUSPENSE.

DURING that long stay in St Malo, waiting for a boat that never came, H.H. and I had two distinct preoccupations. His was the possibility —or improbability—of another boat coming in. Mine was the non-arrival of Dominie's landing licence. I had written for an application form, had filled it in and sent it off to the Animal Health Division of the Ministry of Agriculture many weeks before, but the postal service was interrupted between France and England and, when I left the South, I had had no letters from home for a very long time. Dominie's permit to set paw in England was lying in some post-bag—in what port of England or France ? I knew how strict were the rules of quarantine in England, the landing licence, the carrying agent who must come to the boat with a cage or kennel, carry the victim ashore in it and convey him to whatever concentration camp had been chosen. Having no landing licence for my Blackness before we left home, I had asked old Doctor Rozier to take blood-tests and then, if they were in every way satis-factory, to give me a health certificate. I held

that French certificate ; had had it officially
stamped by the *Mairie*, and was hoping that
these papers would suffice until we reached an
English port.

My first walk, on the morning after our arrival,
was to the office of the Southern Railway down
on the quay. Early as I was, I met H.H.
despondently trudging away from it.

" No news of a boat. May have to wait
here for weeks—and then not get one," he said
to me heavily. " Every boat at Dunkerque."

" I'm going to see about Dominie," I told
him. Each of us full of our own particular
preoccupation.

I asked to see the Manager, and an old Scot
with a keen grey eye presently appeared. He
listened sympathetically to my explanation of
the non-arrival of Dominie's landing licence,
and then shook his head mournfully.

" Ye'll have to leave him heerre," he said
firmly. " No dog is pairmeeted to embarrrrk
withoot his licence. We shall have to send him
on afterrr ye."

With tremulous hands I spread out Dominie's
French certificate, but, to my horror and
indignation, he would not even look at it.

" The rrregulations arrre vurry strrrict," he
said sadly. " Puir little mon," caressing the
head of my Blackness who cowered and looked
wildly at me. " I regret, Ma'am, that I canna
break them under any cirrrrrcumstances."

One recognises sincerity—and finality—in a
voice. I knew that this old man was sorry

for me and for my puppy, but I also felt the
futility of battering a block of granite with
words.

"Therre was a Pomerrranian and an Alsatian
turned off the boat that went yesterday because
theirr paperrs werre not in orrder," he told me,
as proof of his statement. Then added : " Ye
ken that werre it possible I should be verra
verra glad to make an exception forr this little
black mon."

" I know you would," I said thickly. " Thank
you so much for granting me an interview without appointment."

Dominie must have been surprised, when we
were alone again, to be suddenly swept up
into my arms, and his nose kissed and kissed
and kissed.

Escape to England and leave him behind to
be 'sent on after me!' Who would remember
a terrified puppy if German tanks suddenly
swept into this town and the inhabitants were
forced to flee ? Never would I leave him—
alive. I still had time to act—and there was
a chance that the licence might yet arrive,
forwarded with my letters. I had telegraphed
our arrival at St Malo to *Mademoiselle*.

A gathering mob of exhausted refugees
swarmed into the town every day and all day,
by train, car, bicycle, or on foot. Many of
them were suffering from shell-shock, and all
became increasingly nervous as the arrival of
boats was rumoured, then denied.

H.H. buttonholed anything that he could

see in Naval uniform and asked it questions that could not be answered. He scanned his daily newspaper more and more anxiously—the Germans were advancing nearer and nearer and our men were retreating towards the coast. With their backs to the sea they would fight to the last man—if they could not be embarked before they were all massacred. Everyone in the hotel thronged the hall to listen to the French and English news ; many of the Belgians, in spite of their anxiety, falling asleep through sheer exhaustion from their terrible experiences. I saw one man, an eminent financier of Brussels, sagging over the arm of his chair like a dead body, save for his congested face ; for his head hung down nearly touching the floor. I watched his friend replace him several times that evening. Those who could find no empty chairs sat on the steps of the staircase, and after a time haggard women slipped sideways and lay asleep against the shoulders of complete strangers. There was one girl who almost unnerved me whenever I saw her — because she had so completely lost her nerve. Then Dominie introduced us ; for, as we passed her chair, she put out a shaking hand to caress his domed head.

" He's lovely," she whispered to me, " you are taking him back to England ? "

She had stabbed me unknowingly and I suppose I must have flinched.

" Oh, I am so sorry," she said, realising with the intuition of the hyper-sensitive that she had somehow wounded me. Then: "Won't you tell me about it?"

"May I?" I said. "Will you come out on the ramparts with us? We are going for our final run before bed."

If I told her my trouble perhaps she might tell me hers. She could not help me, but there was some chance that I could help her.

She was very sweet and sympathetic about the Blackness, and then, without being asked, she jerked out her own story. She had been a member of the Anglo-American Ambulance Corps in Paris. She was suffering from an acute appendix. An immediate operation had been arranged for in Paris—then, suddenly, Paris was evacuated and she was sent to Calais to be shipped to a London hospital. When she reached Calais the town was being bombarded, and she was sent back to Paris to take from there a train to Boulogne. By the time she arrived at Boulogne the Germans were bombarding that port also, and she was forced to travel back again to Paris. The same thing happened at Le Havre and Cherbourg. She had been travelling ceaselessly for days and nights in agony, standing in gigantic queues, jostled by crowds, pushed into overcrowded railway carriages, unable to get food or drink while the trains were stranded for hours and hours in sidings, fainting amid a mob of refugees so thick that it held up her insensible body with its pressure; reviving slowly, to be tortured again by that inner agony which could only be alleviated now by the knife of a London surgeon.

"Do you think there will be a boat to-morrow?" she asked me with shaking lips and sweat streaming down her face.

"The Jersey boat is still running," I replied, quite truthfully, and added, with less truth (for I had been told that it only ran once a fortnight and had left two days before): "It may come in at any moment." I had to try to stop that awful shaking.

"Bed for you now," I said, telling her the number of my room in case of need. "And surely you have some remedy to dull those paroxysms of pain?"

"The English doctor in Paris gave me a wonderful prescription," she told me despairingly, "but the English chemist here has gone, and none of the French ones can understand the English prescription. They don't know the names of the drugs. Endless cocktails are the only things that quiet the pain and my nerves."

A dark-skinned man with the blue-tinged lips and straight black hair of a half-caste Indian came up to her as we approached the hotel.

"He has been so marvellously kind in looking after me since I left Paris," she whispered. "He saw me faint, and took charge. Good-night—and I'm sure, somehow, that it will be all right about your little Dominie. Good-night, old boy." She patted the Blackness and went with her dusky escort into the American bar.

H.H. was playing patience in a corner of the hall. The sight of that huge quiet frame steadied me at once.

Pray God that I may have the same controlled nerves, the same calm cheerfulness if I reach that age. He was wonderful. And so good to Dominie and me.

CHAPTER XVII.

THE LAST LINK WITH HOME.

LIFE in St Malo during that period of waiting had, for me, an unreality which closely resembled a fever-dream. Waiting for a boat that might never come ; wondering what would happen to this seething mass of refugees if it did not, and shaping plans for the escape of H.H., Dominie, and myself if the Germans arrived before the boat, agitated my very tired mind which never ceased to worry also over the non-arrival of Dominie's landing licence. I haunted the hotel office asking constantly if there was a letter for me. I received a telegram from *Mademoiselle* asking to be reassured as to our safety. But nothing more.

The big English Provost-Marshal of the town was wonderfully kind to us all. He encouraged exhausted refugees with his assurance that a boat of some sort would surely come in to-morrow, and, when it did not, the next day. He exercised lonely officers' wives (whose husbands were fighting at Dunkerque—or had been fighting in Calais) along the ramparts. He led nervous old gentlemen into the American bar and made them happy with heartening drinks. He was here, there, and everywhere with his Military Police—a fine body of men.

" What about that black chap of yours ? " he asked of me, indicating Dominie. I told him the story.

" Come along with me to the office of the Southern Railway," he said at the end of it. " I'm sure we can fix this up."

I had no hope in my heart, but we went, and once more talked with the Scots Manager.

" Can't be done, Sirrr," repeated that old man with a reproachful look at me. " Do ye ken the peenalty forr the Captain if he allows a dog to embarrrrk withoot a licence ? A fine of a hundrred pounds—and he loses his ship." I looked sorrowfully at the P.M. who seemed staggered by this reply.

" There's a ship comin' in to-morrow night, maybe," said the old man, bowing himself back into his busy office.

A ship coming in to-morrow !

" Look here, Lady Fortescue," said the P.M. on our way back to the hotel. " Leave your puppy with my Police. Soldiers love dogs and they'd be awfully good to him. They've already got the care of an Alsatian and a Pomeranian who were pushed off the last boat because they hadn't got their landing licences. When all their licences arrive we can put the three dogs on the next boat. My advice to you is, leave your dog here and get out, with that old man, to-morrow."

I stopped dead and faced him.

"Look here," I said, staring him in the eyes. "Answer me as man to man. If it is so urgent that we get out to-morrow, *will there be another boat?*"

He reddened and looked very unhappy, then answered bluntly—

"Well—since you put it like that, I think it's extremely unlikely."

"Thank you," I said. "Now I know what I must do."

We walked back to the hotel in silence. In the hall, my usual inquiry: "Are there any letters for me?"

"*Non, Madame.*"

Dominie and I went upstairs to our room. I rang the bell, and when the chamber-maid came I asked her if she would find my chauffeur and send him up to my room. Presently there was a knock at my door. It was Jean. Before I could speak he said—

"I have been trying to find *Madame* to tell her that I shall be obliged to start on my homeward journey to-day. It is the last day of the month, and my petrol coupons will not be available after to-day. I have been trying to arrange at the *Mairie* here for extra coupons, but they will not allow them. I must drive very fast all day and all through the night with what petrol I have until I reach the garage of a friend who will give me some more. I have friends in many garages, but I have never before come so far north as this."

"Oh—Jean!" was all that I could say at

first. Then: "Make up your bill, Jean, and then start at once. You were wonderful to leave your wife and children to come with me. Much as I want to keep you until we know whether or not we can get a ship, I can't risk your being stuck here and perhaps taken prisoner."

"I do not want to leave, *Madame*," he said with feeling, "but this question of petrol —the journey took so much longer than we had hoped—we came so far——"

"Go now, Jean," I urged him, "and return quickly with your bill." I scrawled a hasty note for him to take to *Mademoiselle*, and I copied out our route to St Malo, to be given to our British Vice-Consul in Cannes for the benefit of other English people who might wish to escape from France, enclosing a letter telling him that St Malo was now the only port left open, though at any moment now that also might be closed. If they should follow our route they must do it at their own risk.

While I was writing, the Blackness had somehow inserted himself into my chair. It is uncanny the way dogs can sense one's misery. Should I push him into Jean's arms and tell him to take my puppy back to *Mademoiselle?* There was still time.

Jean knocked again at the door. I paid him the tremendous bill for that long journey through France, and made the sum bigger than it need have been. If I could have doubled

it I would have done so joyfully. I gave him
my letters, with the request that he should
place them, himself, into the hands of *Mademoiselle* and our Vice-Consul. He put them
carefully into his pocket-book, stowed it away,
and then stood holding his chauffeur's cap
looking at me mournfully.

" Oh, Jean," I said, " you were my last
link with home "—already I had put him into
the past, he had so nearly gone—" God bless you
always for coming with me, Jean—and now go
—go quickly. I don't want you to see me cry."

Jean was already crying : " I shall never
forget *Madame*," he said, and then he went.

I drew the ruby velvet curtains across the
windows to shut out the blazing sunlight and
lay down on the great bed. There was a sudden
flump by my side and something silky and
soft scrabbled itself closer and closer to me.
It was the Blackness. With a great sigh he
laid his head on my chest. I put my arms
round him, hugging him closer yet—and then,
for the first time since I had left home, came
the relief of tears. . . .

There came a knock at my door. A muffled
" Come in." H.H. towered in the doorway.
His glance swept the shadowed room and
rested upon Dominie and me, huddled together
on the bed. . . .

" You needn't think I'm going to leave you
both. Not on your life ! " he said unexpectedly.
" I'm here ! Ha ! Ha ! " and withdrew, shutting
the door softly behind him.

CHAPTER XVIII.

REPRIEVED.

THE next morning Dominie and I came down-stairs early. When we reached the last landing which overlooked the hall I saw the usual crowd of people, but this morning they were sitting about in depressed silence. Standing amidst them was the big Provost-Marshal. Suddenly he caught sight of me and called out—

"Lady Fortescue, you are the only person in this hotel who will be glad of my news. The boat's cancelled."

"Oh, thank God!" I said, catching up my struggling Blackness into my arms. "Reprieved!"

Despite his disappointment and anxiety because the boat was cancelled, H.H.'s face was just one big grin when he saw the radiance on mine, for he, also, had learned to love Dominie.

"Now I've got time to do things," I babbled to him. "I shall send a reply-paid telegram to the Ministry of Agriculture asking them to cable to the Southern Railway giving per-mission for my Blackness to embark."

H.H. shook his head dubiously. "Your

telegram will never leave France at such a time, my dear," he said sadly. "Everyone's mind is concentrated upon Dunkerque. The congestion on the line must be terrific."

"I think I know how I can get it through," I replied, "I know my French. If I make my reply-paid terribly expensive they will be impressed, because nobody in France ever pays for anything in advance, especially something they may never get."

So Dominie and I toiled up to the General Post Office to send our telegram. We queued up in the *Gendarmerie* where every foreign telegram had to be examined, with the passport and *carte d'identité* of the sender, and then stamped—or refused. For once the heat, the stench of garlic, human exertion, and hot, unwashen refugees, could not sicken me. I was too happy. The Chief of Police recognised Dominie and me—we had visited his office often with telegrams to *Mademoiselle*—and took our telegram out of turn. He read it and raised his eyebrows involuntarily as he read 200 francs for a reply, then bowed me out very respectfully. This heartened me. The same reception was given to my telegram and me in the General Post Office. Somehow I felt sure that telegram would get through.

The next two days were very difficult to bear—for everybody. One wife of an officer of the Gordon Highlanders, who, we knew, had been outnumbered in Calais and had put up a gallant fight, spent her time peeling potatoes for the refugees' kitchen until her fingers were blistered. The atmosphere of St Malo was becoming more and more electric. When Dominie and I took our nightly walk in the secret Square of our discovery, we found hundreds of wooden wheel-barrows piled up mysteriously in a dark corner. Very odd, but I, at anyrate, knew what they were for. In the morning I met the P.M. walking alone.

" You have a nice little stock of wheel-barrows in readiness," I remarked jauntily. " To fetch sand from the seashore, of course." He had got used to me by this time, so merely answered—

" You've said it. They're getting very near."

" If the bombardment starts to-night," I said, " must Dominie and I descend from our fourth floor ? And, if so, where do we go ? "

" Inside these fat fortified walls there are splendid shelters, but——" and he looked nervously at me, " I'm afraid dogs are not allowed inside them."

" Very well," I replied, " then we will find ' a better 'ole ' somewhere."

A delightful Naval Commander in the Intelligence had joined us. He was the chief of Dominie's new friends, and had once, by his gentleness and love of beasts, tamed a baby tiger-cub for his own. He understood.

" We'll go and find a place, now," he said quietly. The P.M. saluted and moved off, and Dominie, the Commander, and I went down to the shore. Here, in a scooped curve of the ramparts he decreed that Dominie and I should lie flat on our faces on the sand, a pillow over our heads and a pencil between my teeth. He did not tell me that that place was completely covered at high tide.

On the morning of the third day we were informed that a boat would come into port at sunset. The answer to my telegram had not yet come. I took my Blackness for endless short walks to make an excuse for leaving and entering the hotel. At first I asked at the office if there was a telephone message for me from the Southern Railway—the dear old Scots Manager had promised, himself, to let me know if the longed-for telegram arrived, but when I had passed the office several times, at not very long intervals, I could not ask any more. I merely lifted my eyebrows, and the sympathetic Frenchwoman at the desk shrugged her shoulders sadly. Suddenly H.H. intervened—

"I've taken a table for luncheon at the restaurant at the end of the street. We are not lunching at the hotel to-day," he said firmly, "and I have invited that poor little woman who is so anxious about her husband in Calais. So you must be there to help me cheer her up. Give Dominie his dinner in your room and then come along."

I had meant to hover round our hotel. I doubt if, left to myself, I should have eaten at all. The look in H.H.'s eyes told me that he knew all this, was prescribing a tonic, and

expected me to take it. I did take it. But
I excused myself early from that luncheon
on the plea of final packing to do and returned
to the hotel.

I was met at the door by a smiling
Manageress.

" I have looked everywhere in the hotel for
Madame. The Manager of the Southern Railway
has telephoned three times for *Madame*. He
has a telegram. . . ."

I fled past her, towing a startled Dominie
after me, rushed to the telephone, rang up the
Southern Railway, and asked for the Manager.
A palpitating pause, and then a slow Scots
voice spoke to me—

" Lady Forrrtescue, I have received this
telegrram from the Meenistry of Agriculture :
' We give pairmeesion forr Lady Forrrtescue's
black Cockerrr spaniel to embarrrrk.' I'm reet
glad to give you the noos, Lady Forrrtescue.
I am that."

" Oh, bless you ! Bless *everybody*," I babbled.
I heard a slow chuckle, and then—

" I'm reet glad it's a' reet," and the click of
the receiver as the old man hung it up.

I must tell H.H. ! I must tell everybody
this wonderful news ! I rushed headlong out
of the hotel, this time ahead of Dominie, who
panted after me on his lead.

" His licence has come ! " I called to officers
old and young drinking coffee with their women
at the little tables outside the hotel, and they
beamed and waved triumphantly to me as I

fled past them. "*Son permis est arrivé!*" I shouted to the luggage-porter, stacking luggage on to a taxi—

"*C'est bien, ça!*" he yelled to my flying form.

H.H. had just paid the bill and was collecting hat and stick when I literally fell upon him—

"It's come! Dominie's licence has come! Isn't it too wonderful?" I gasped.

H.H. raised both arms into the air, brandishing hat and stick—

"My dear! How splendid! How perfectly splendid!

"HA! **HA**!"

Everyone in the restaurant and the street turned to see what superman could emit a sound like that; Dominie, infected with our joyous excitement, barked and danced round the life-size wooden figure of a *chef* bearing a steaming dish which advertised the restaurant; tangled me up in his lead so that the *chef* and I fell into each other's arms; H.H. disentangled the three of us and set up the wooden figure in its place; and eventually we all skipped back to the hotel leaving the mystified *clientèle* of that restaurant smiling sympathetically and shaking their heads over ' those mad English.'

CHAPTER XIX.

FAREWELL, FRANCE.

EVERYONE in St Malo had been packed up for days, save for night-gear, when they had any—and, in some cases, toothbrushes—so as to be ready to leave at any moment should a boat come in. We were now ordered to take what luggage we had, early, to the office of the Southern Railway where the mob of people who had been waiting to get away must book places on the boat and go through many formalities. Some of them had neglected to go to the Consular office to have their *départ* authorised and an embarkation paper given to them, and these fled thither now in a panic.

The Naval Commander who had befriended Dominie and me suggested that we give Dominie one last run on the shore—the only place where he could be unleashed—before taking our baggage down to the quay. A thick luminous mist shrouded sand and sea, muffling sound in a mysterious ghostly way. We walked on and on towards where the sea should be, but the tide had receded so far that the stretch of hard wet sand seemed endless, and we heard no sigh of waves beyond us. The Blackness had completely disappeared. The moment that I unleashed him he had a fit of tearums, rushing madly round and round in a wide circle, eyes glaring, banner-ears and feathered legs flying, then, catching up a bit of seaweed in his laughing mouth, the liberated Blackness tore away and vanished into silvery space. I called him, but there was no sight or sound of him.

" He has rushed down to the sea to have a paddle," I said, " I'll go and find him." And leaving the Commander with the Scots officer's little wife who had come with us, I ran forward. Suddenly I saw a very wet Cocker laughing up at me. *He* had found the sea at anyrate. We turned together to make our way back to our friends, but now *they* had completely vanished. I called and my voice seemed to die after travelling a yard. This was almost uncanny. I called again. Then I remembered that once, up in the High Alps, one of our company had gone, alone, for a long mountain walk. A thick fog descended and *Mademoiselle* and I, growing anxious, had fixed a lantern on an alpenstock on our plateau ; we had whistled, shouted, blown a horn (made from the horn of a mountain goat), but there had been no reply. Then I had let forth a weird kind of home-made yodel, and, to our astonishment, Dominie had thrown back his head and given almost an exact imitation of this howl, rendered more weird and penetrating by a canine voice. Our friend heard that howl and was guided by Dominie back to the plateau. I let forth the same specimen of howl now, and, as before, Dominie copied it, not once but thrice. A woolly shout—from somewhere—impossible for me to locate from whence it came, but this time I followed the Blackness, who nosed out our friends by scent alone.

"Extraordinary!" I said. "We had completely lost you in this sea-fog. Do you think— oh! Do you think that it is helping them at Dunkerque?"

"That is a harmless question that I *can* answer," replied the Commander. "It is. I telephoned this morning and was told that the weather conditions were the same as here. The fog was helping to conceal the movements of troops and boats."

"Oh, thank God!" the officer's little wife exclaimed in one breath with me.

Back at the hotel, someone contrived to get a taxi, which we shared with some others, and the men of the party hauled out and heaved in the heterogeneous collection of hand-baggage, packing the women into any vacant spaces left. The Blackness climbed up on to the top of us, where he sat, panting triumphantly, with a look of assurance which plainly said: "I, also, have a landing licence. I have as much right to travel on that ship as any one of you."

We stood in queues inside the building of the Southern Railway, stewing in a fug; when exhausted, we sat upon our baggage; when nearly stifled, we took it in turns to keep a place

in the queue while someone fought their way
out-of-doors for a stroll on the quay.

The fuss over Dominie was still not over.
Apparently he had to be registered as a parcel,
and there was a special office which performed
this feat. He and I pushed through crowds
and crept under barriers in search of this place,
and, when we found it, needless to say, there
was no one inside it. However, the quest
gave us something to do, so that if more
badgered we were less bored than the rest of
the waiting crowd. At length this formality
was accomplished, and then I was told that on
the boat he would not be allowed in my cabin,
if I got one, but would be obliged to travel in
charge of the cook. Knowing my Blackness,
I felt that if the cook were a kind cook he might
even enjoy the voyage—*if* cooking was being
done ; but as we were extremely likely to be
bombed, bombarded, or torpedoed, I was
resolved that he should stay with me, even
if I, also, shared the cook's galley. But this I
confided to no one.

The scrum of people was so dense that no
official noticed a little black Cocker wriggling
through the crowd by the side of his mistress,
and, during our long wait in St Malo when his
fate hung in the balance, he had made many
friends among refugees of all nations who, by
this time, knew his story ; so that sympathetic
room was made for my little Blackness, who
received many swift caresses and congratulations
as he writhed and batted his way up the gang-

way, across the deck, down a long corridor—
and into my cabin, for, miraculously as it seemed
to me, I actually had a so-called *cabine-de-luxe*
reserved for me. As we had been the earliest
arrivals after the departure of the last boat,
and had put down our names at once for the
next, both H.H. and I were given cabins, to
our great content. Mine had a door-handle
that fell off at intervals and rolled into a corner
under my bunk, and, for the first half-hour
before we sailed, I frequently had to lie on
my stomach and make swimming movements
to find it, getting grimier every time. At
length, in irritation, I bolted my door, whereupon a hefty stewardess hammered heavily
upon it for admittance—

" You must not bolt yourself in, Madam.
It is very dangerous. If we are mined or torpedoed, how can anyone get at you ? "

I explained why I had done it, and she
struggled, ineffectually, to arrange the door-
handle. " You must just hook your door half
open," she said at length. " I'm sorry we haven't
got a curtain, but, with the light out, I don't
think anyone would see you in bed. Pity it's
just opposite the door."

" And my door is just opposite the
MESSIEURS," I said with a little grimace.

She smiled broadly, and, just as she was
departing, caught sight of a little black blot
at the foot of my bed.

" I hope the little dog is clean in his habits,
Madam," she said severely. " Dogs are

not——" She got no further, for I burst in with, " I assure you he's as clean as—as *you* are. In fact, we don't know what we're going to do without a grass plot and seclusion."

She looked at Dominie and saw two appealing amber eyes and an apology for a tail with a tiny feather of hair on the end of it that flickered insinuatingly. She melted.

" He's a beautiful little black fellow," she said as she went out of the cabin. Dominie and I gave a simultaneous wooffff of relief.

Foreseeing fierce formalities, I had brought his dinner ready prepared in a little tin pot in his own knapsack, enough for two meals, so that we could hide in our cabin and ask no favours of anyone ; and I planned to exercise him on deserted decks while the conquering passengers devoured the first meal served in the dining-saloon and the vanquished stood in queues and sat on the stairway eyeing them with hate and awaiting the second, third, fourth, or fifth service. H.H.—his bulk had told—was among the Conquerors. He had hoped, by going down early, to reserve two places, but, once in, it was quite impossible to get out again to find me, and therefore, in spite of his unavailing protests, someone slipped into the place he wanted to reserve for me. So there he sat, chewing the cud of mortification.

Meanwhile, Dominie and I scrambled up stairways on to decks, slipped between funnels and skated round stanchions in search of inspiration. Near the deck-house, we came upon a tall figure muffled in a greatcoat. He accosted me cheerily. Horrors! It was the Captain.

" I was just giving my dog a little exercise while the decks are empty and he can't be a nuisance to anybody," I said breathlessly.

" Your dog? I see no dog," he replied, looking me straight in the eyes. Those eyes of his had a gleam in them and his lips twitched ever so slightly.

What a DARLING! Dominie and I pattered joyfully on our way.

Somewhere about ten o'clock that night we got into the saloon and picked up the crumbs that had fallen from our predecessors' tables.

We could not be convoyed, but our dear dirty old khaki-coloured boat had a magnetic belt for our protection. We were neither bombed, nor torpedoed, nor bombarded that night, and the sea was so calm that one could hardly believe that the ship was moving. Dominie's bottle of water which, having no cork, I had placed in the washing-basin, never even rattled. Nevertheless I had prepared for the very worst, putting on my waterproof ski-ing trousers and tunic and calling the stewardess to dress me up in those complicated lumps of cork that I had found in my cabin. I had put my few treasures, important papers, and some consolatory charcoal biscuits for Dominie, into a weatherproof boy-scout's knapsack so as to have my arms free to hold my Blackness, but those blocks of cork made it impossible to adjust this on my back, and the stewardess advised me to sling it over my elbow : " Then, if you find that the weight of the bag and the little dog make you sink, you can let slip the bag." If she had said ' the dog,' I think murder would have been done, but, being an English stewardess, she realised that Dominie was of more value than many jewels.

" Do you take off your clothes when you go to bed ? " I asked.

" I haven't had my clothes off for weeks," replied the gallant woman, " and no one on this ship has stopped working, night or day, since Friday. Be sure and slide gently into the water and don't jump, or the lifebelt will jerk upwards and break your neck. Good-night, Madam," she said in parting.

I learned next day that her final advice and benediction, heard plainly all down the corridor because my door would not shut, gave neighbouring passengers anything but a good night.

CHAPTER XX.

THE CARRYING-AGENT.

NOBODY knew into which English port we might be able to enter. I had merely telegraphed : " Leaving for England to-day," to Messrs Cox & King's, the carrying-agents who were to collect my Dominie, leaving it to them to find out our port, the day and hour of arrival. Their only clue would be the name of the place from which the telegram was sent.

All the decks were crowded next morning. Even shell-shocked women who had been bombed and machine-gunned as they fled before the German advance, tottered from their cabins to catch the first glimpse of England.

A blur on the horizon revealed itself slowly as the mainland, with a darker strip of land before it—the Isle of Wight. We were coming into Southampton. My heart beat thickly with a great emotion. We had reached home —at last.

But, oh no ! we had not. Not yet. It was not to be as simple as that. Suddenly we realised that the boat had glided to a standstill. Some minor hitch, no doubt. I lit a cigarette.

H.H.'s great body swivelled round and his eyebrows shot up, but he said nothing.

It was nine o'clock in the morning when we anchored opposite the Isle of Wight, which looked within easy swimming distance. At half-past ten the boat was still immovable and the passengers were becoming restive and inquisitive. The Captain, constantly questioned, supposed that we were before our time. This answer satisfied some, but H.H. and I exchanged sceptical glances, though we did not put our suspicions into words.

Twelve noon. Our position still the same, but by this time H.H. could sit still no longer and started a tour of inquiry. He returned to me looking grim.

" The Solent has been mined," he said in an undertone. " They have to clean up before we can get in. Those are mine-sweepers over there," indicating a line of small craft in the direction of Portsmouth.

A distant throbbing in the air which gradually intensified until it was unmistakably the engine of an aeroplane which soon became visible making for Portsmouth. A sudden burst of gun-fire from the coast told us that the aeroplane was none of ours.

" It really will be rather hard," I thought, " if, after such a journey, we get bombed to the bottom within sight of England."

But we were not. Our extraordinary luck held, and, although we were imprisoned on that ship, with a very scant supply of food and water, for ten hours of suspense, we came safely into port at seven o'clock that evening.

Amid the sailors, porters, Customs officials, soldiers, and loiterers awaiting us on the quay as we sidled slowly up to it, I noticed a small slightly-built man, hatless, wearing a light grey suit. It was his pleasant upturned face and eager eyes that attracted and held mine. Curiously enough, his eyes were not scanning the faces of the passengers, but searched along a lower level of the deck. We drew in nearer yet, and, interested by this particular man, I continued to watch him, wondering for what he sought. His eyes travelled along from the bows of the boat, and then amidships, where I was standing, I noticed that his gaze became suddenly riveted. His knees bent, he leaned a little forward, smiled all over his face, and pursed his mouth into a whistle.

I looked down, and, poked through the deck rails, was the head of my Blackness, pink tongue lolling, banner ears blowing in the wind, excited over yet another new experience.

I had written a rather absurd letter to the Manager of Messrs Cox & King's telling him that I was bringing back to England with me a very loving but terribly nervous little Cocker ; that I dreaded for him the six months enforced quarantine, and, more than all, the railway journey to the kennels. My dog would be shut inside a cage, which would be pushed into a luggage van, and, owing to the war-disorganised traffic, he would probably remain there for

forty-eight hours or more. I pleaded with that
Manager that, if it were humanly possible,
he would beg, borrow, or steal a car, lorry
or motor-bus, and the petrol with which to
propel it, and that he would send a dog-loving
man to collect my puppy, my luggage, and me.
This must be the ambassador from Cox &
King's. Already he had spied my Blackness
and had no eyes for anyone else.

A great hand rested on my shoulder. I
looked blindly up. It was H.H.

" Six months passes in no time. He'll be
all right. Dogs are extraordinarily adaptable,"
said the big man with the understanding heart.

The gangway was let down and the little
agent sped lightly up it and struggled through
the crowd to my side.

" Lady Fortescue ? " he inquired, and in a
moment he was bending over the Blackness,
whispering encouragement and fondling his
banner ears. To my happiness, Dominie was
not afraid of him.

" We'll stay here quietly with him till everyone gets off the boat. Then I'll get the cage
and carry him ashore in it," he whispered to
me as though afraid the Blackness might hear.
" I've got a car. The Manager made a great
point of it, and said I must somehow do the
impossible. We have orders to deliver the
little dog to the kennels, and Your Ladyship
wherever you want to go afterwards."

All through my life I have found the world
to be full of the most wonderful people.

I cannot write about part of the next hour. There was one bright moment.

At the foot of the gangway stood two petty officers examining the passports of passengers as they filed down it. When it came to my turn, one of them glanced at my passport and then smiled at me, saying: "Lady Fortescue, I have waited here for hours just to see you and to say, 'Thank you.' I was privileged to review your first book for 'Punch.'"

"Oh, bless you!" I cried. "What a lovely welcome to England," and we shook hands very warmly. Just for a moment he made me forget those goggling amber eyes, and feathered feet scrabbling frantically against imprisoning wire.

Interminable delays while papers were examined and baggage searched by the Customs. It was growing dusk. Could we reach those kennels, on the other side of London, before darkness fell?

A voice in my ear, "I'm afraid, Your Ladyship, we'll never make Hertfordshire to-night. There are so many guarded bridges to hold us up—and there's the black-out. Neither I nor the driver know the way very well, and it's difficult reading maps in the dark. We might easily be shot at if we didn't hear an order to stop. I'd rather not risk it if Your Ladyship would consent to stay the night in Southampton and make an early start to-morrow morning."

H.H., whose baggage was already in the boat-train, had come up to say good-bye to me and overheard this speech.

" I'll get out my luggage and stay in South-
ampton too and see you through," he announced.

" You'll do no such thing," I contradicted
him vehemently. " It's wonderful of you to
think of it, but your duty is to get home as
soon as possible to your anxious family. I'm
on English soil now, perfectly safe, and able to
look after myself. Bless you ! Good-bye ! "

" You really mean it ? I'm perfectly willing
to stay."

" You've suffered enough from Dominie and
me. Go home now and be at peace."

He crushed my hand in his great palm and
hurried to his carriage, waving his hat to me
before he got into it. I waved back. There
went a faithful friend, a very gallant gentleman.

" I've been with the little chap while you
were going through the Customs, Your Ladyship. He's quite quiet now. He's had some
water to drink and I've given him some of
those charcoal biscuits you said he was so fond
of. Later on he shall have some supper. Now,
which hotel would Your Ladyship like to
stay at ? "

It was the little carrying-agent. I looked
at him wildly.

"Don't, oh don't send me to a grand hotel.
I should die if I had to spend to-night alone
in an hotel. I've lost my home in France—
and my friends out there—and now I've lost
my puppy. I couldn't bear to be alone to-night.
Surely you are married ? I'm certain you've
got a cosy little house with rambler roses

crawling over it and a kind wife who will let me come there and sleep on the floor. I've got my camping rug and pillow. I only want an egg for supper—and—oh! a cup of tea and someone to be kind to me to-night."

Though naturally somewhat startled by this burst of incoherence, I could see that he did not think me mad.

He looked shy and a little apprehensive, but always kind and sympathetic—

"Well, I am married, Your Ladyship, but ours is just a very simple little home and——"

"Oh! just what I need to-night. Please take me there," I pleaded.

"Well, I could run across the road and telephone to the wife—to warn her so to speak —we have to have a 'phone to get orders through for the firm."

"Oh, go and telephone! Please go. I don't mind how long I wait here," I assured him. And he went.

They were divine to me, that family. They *did* live in a pretty little house with rambler roses clambering about it, and had a cosy cat, and their schoolboy son turned out of his bed so that I might have it, and I had a delicious new-laid egg for supper, and toast and home-made jam, and heavenly hot tea. And, later, when I was tucked up in that little bed, a lovely cup of hot cocoa was brought to me with such kind and comforting care. I shall never forget that dear little family.

CHAPTER XXI.

LOVELY ENGLISH REALITY.

We made an early start next day, the Blackness, in his hated cage, in the back of the car by my side. I felt exactly like Rip van Winkle must have felt, awaking in his own land after a sleep of a hundred years, for nothing that I had known was now familiar. Guarded bridges, barricaded roads, sand-bagged shops, great blocks of flats where once had stood old houses, ribbon-development-building along wide by-pass roads cutting across country. Tanks, armoured cars, dispatch riders roaring along on motor-bicycles, army lorries, squads of marcning soldiers, aeroplanes throbbing overhead—and no sign-posts anywhere. Even when we left the towns and main thoroughfares to pass along wooded lanes we came upon strange military surprises amid this June beauty ; a hidden camp ; or a big gun poking its ugly snout through the trees. After some hours of this I felt that only a meal of roast beef and Yorkshire pudding with two vegs. and horse-radish sauce, followed by a fruit pie of some sort, and then, probably, execrable coffee, could convince me that I was back in England.

We reached the Hertfordshire kennels at last. Lovely kennels with big grass runs. The Blackness had a palatial wooden hut reserved for him and a bed built up from the floor to avoid draughts, and the kind kennel-man greeted him as " My Beautiful." But we won't talk about that any more. . . .

The proprietor of the kennels, disabled in the last war, told me that I could be immediately useful as interpreter for the French wounded soldiers who, after the evacuation of Dunkerque, had been hurriedly placed in so many hospitals in Hertfordshire and elsewhere. As a race, modern languages have never been our strong point, and, he said, the *poilus* were suffering from homesickness almost more than from wounds. If I would only combine a visit to Dominie with one to the local hospital, the doctors and nurses, as well as the French soldiers, would bless me. Had I not been laden with that odd assortment of baggage, I would have turned the car back to South-ampton and have gone at once, in his, to the hospital. Even the *thought* of seeing, and speaking again with my beloved *poilus;* of still being able to help and comfort them, helped and comforted me in that sad hour. I promised to come over — if I could *get* over—as soon as possible, and then I drove away.

I had not told any of my family or friends that I was on my way to England because, when I started, I thought it extremely improbable that at that late hour I could get out of France. And even if I succeeded in finding an open port I knew they would worry over my attempting so risky an adventure at such a time, and that I should be unable to reassure them as to my safety.

Silence was best, and, because the postal communications between England and France had been for so long delayed and deranged, this would not seem sinister. I intended, if at last I reached my native land, just to walk into my brother's house, sure of a glad welcome from him and my sister-in-love and a rapturous greeting from their four little daughters.

My ' surprise ' arrival fell rather flat, because all, save the children's beloved Nannie, were out, and on the hall table was a pile of letters re-addressed to me from France. I had given my brother's address for my letters to be sent on, thinking that they would arrive long after I did in those days of leisurely transmission. But I had been so long on my journey that the first batch had already awaited me for some days. Consequently the family had had a shrewd suspicion that soon I should be with them, and the children had been competing to answer door and telephone bell-rings for days. All this was told me by their Nannie after she had regained breath from my first hug. When the carrying-agent and his pal, the chauffeur, had carried my luggage into the hall, and I had paid as much of my debt to these kind men as could be paid in money, and had bidden them good-bye, I was taken upstairs to the lovely room prepared for me long since. One of its two big windows looked out across a queer-cut yew-hedge to the beautiful old church, and the other overlooked a vast green garden through which a little singing stream meandered lazily under great trees to lush meadows beyond. Here was the England that I had known. In this huge Rectory with its stables and endless outhouses sprawling round it, I felt again the happy atmosphere of my youth, spent in just such another house, though, fortunately, built on a smaller scale. Here were the same long corridors, the scratched paint — I saw dear familiar furniture from our old home, pictures that our youthful eyes had stared at in interested wonder, photographs of our family, and flowers everywhere. The children's room was strewn with toys and picture-books, a shoe flung here, a grubby sock there. Their Nannie caught up objects and little garments, putting them in their place as we toured the rooms talking happily. The children would soon be home from school. Their Daddie and Mummie were somewhere in the parish. How excited everyone would be that I had come home at last !

A hubbub in the hall. The baby spied me on the stairs. " Auntie Win is HOME ! " Onslaught, triumphant shouts. Everyone wanting to show me house, garden, pets, toys, *now, at once*, and to tell me all their news in a breath ; introductions to dancing, barking dogs, a little

Cairn—an old friend—and two lovely golden Cockers whom I had never before seen. I was so thankful that they were not black. . . .

The arrival of my brother and my sister-in-love distracted thoughts that had flown to a certain concentration camp.

" Hullo, darling ! Then you're here at last," quietly, from the beloved brother with eyes that spoke his gladness.

" Win, darling ! How lovely ! " from his wife.

" If you children don't go upstairs at once and get ready, the beef will be cold ! " from their Nannie.

Beef ! Beef ! Beautiful British Beef ! Followed by a redcurrant and raspberry pie ; and then GOOD coffee, enjoyed in a huge cool rose-filled drawing-room with French windows opening on to green lawns, and the smell of lime blossom warmed by June sunshine blowing in to us.

The strange, cold dream was ended. This was reality. Lovely English reality.

CHAPTER XXII.

'ET TU, BRUTE.'

NEVERTHELESS, awakening next day in that cool English bedroom, putting out a hand to feel for a silky head and finding none ; answering a knock at the door with the customary " *Entrez !* " and seeing the children's blue-clad, golden-haired Nannie carrying in my coffee, instead of my Italian *bonne* wearing her primrose-yellow overall with dark hair bound by a scarlet scarf, was, for a second, very bewildering. For the interval of anxiety and unrest since I had left my home in Provence had begun to fade while I ' nested ' (*Mademoiselle's* expression for settling oneself in), and when my clothes were unpacked and put away, and my writing things arranged on the large table provided for my work, I began to lose the giddy sensation of standing upon a revolving stage while changing scenery whirled past me. Shifting impermanence was replaced by the safety and solidity of a comfortable bed in an English Rectory, *my brother's Rectory*, and when I awoke, for the first time for many months I did not find that I had been lying with a stiff body, fists and teeth clenched, bracing myself in my sleep for what might come. When my senses were fully awake, it seemed that I had just floated from the jessamine and lilies of my home in Provence to the roses and honeysuckle of my beloved brother's home in England— with no heart-rending interval between. Only a bruised body, mind, and spirit, reminded me of that, and the lack of that waggling warmness on my bed.

The sense of security remained, but the bewilderment increased as I strove to adjust my behaviour to the changes wrought by time in my nieces. Babies no more, the youngest would soon be six years old, the eldest was nearly seventeen. All four of them had distinct personalities now, and wills and minds of their own. They had a great deal to say to me and many questions to ask.

I was shown the guinea-pigs and the rabbits, and was informed of marriages that had been arranged or consummated and of the dates that families were expected. I was shown school examination papers and realised, with shame, that I could have hardly answered one question satisfactorily. I saw the four girls start off in the morning for their school, slinging their gas-masks over their shoulders with gestures of matter-of-fact boredom, and I thought of our region of the South of France where no gas-masks had ever been seen until *Mademoiselle* ordered yards of Turkish towelling and asked us to contrive make-shift masks for the village children, like square sponge-bags

with an oblong seeing-space cut out wherein
we sewed strips of talc.

Mademoiselle—and France! I had left so
much of my heart over there that my thoughts
could not be held in England. I was for ever
picturing familiar scenes which must be taking
place at certain hours; forced to fill in blank
spaces of the canvas by imagination alone,
since there was now no letters, telegrams, or
newspapers coming from France. My own
letters to *Mademoiselle* were returned to me
by the English authorities, marked ' NO SERVICE.'
At that time I was only anxious for the health
of *Mademoiselle*, lest she should kill herself
by overwork for the French Army, for I still
shared the certainty of all the high officials,
both French and English, in the South of
France that Italy would not come into
the war.

And then, suddenly, she stabbed France in
the back, and those thoughts of mine became
anguished and the visions of peace became
nightmare-dreams of war.

Had I believed in the possibility of war
between France and Italy, should I ever
have had the heart to leave those pathetic
peasants who relied so much upon our help
and comfort—to leave *Mademoiselle*—in danger?
What would now happen to those dear people,
to that little place of peace? We were so near
the frontier that in five minutes Italian aeroplanes could roar overhead dropping death and
destruction; so near to the coast that long-

distance shells could shatter our houses. Half the men and boys of our village were Italian, many of them husbands and sons of French-women. They would be herded, now, in con-centration camps and their women and young children left to struggle with this hideous life alone.

No! I do not think that I could have found it in my heart to leave them in such distress, even though mine were torn and tortured for England and my own people.

Well—the matter had been decided for me ; and it is mere cowardice to look back, to waste one's vital spirit on 'IF's ' when one has taken a decisive step. Here there must surely be work that I could do for my country, and, thank God, I had already been asked to help with the French wounded in England.

I became feverishly anxious to get to my French soldiers, and found out, to my joy, that three of the wards of a hospital nearby were full of them. My brother visited the English soldiers in the hospital twice a week and thought that I might drive there with him if this could be arranged. Impulsively I rang up at once, but was informed that " so many of the local ladies were anxious to practise their French on the soldiers, who were some of them badly wounded and all of them very tired after the experience of Dunkerque, that visiting had had to be forbidden. I protested that I had become almost French after ten years lived in France ; that I talked French fluently ; that I had worked with the French Army since the beginning of the war and felt sure that I, homesick for France as they were, could comfort and interest those stranded *poilus* a little. I was told that if ' an outsider ' were admitted, there would be trouble with the excluded local ladies.

RED TAPE. Already it was entangling my eager feet. I resolved to kick them loose and run straight up to London where the French Embassy would provide me with sharp scissors wherewith to cut myself free. Then I would march straight into that hospital, armed with an official *laisser passer*, to the wards containing the wounded French who needed me.

Someone once told me that he dared not give me advice because, for me, " there was never an instant between decision and action." In this case there had to be an interval of eight hours, because I telephoned to the hospital in the evening and therefore was obliged to wait until the Green Line Coach left for London next morning. But when it did go, I went with it.

I sent in my papers and credentials at the French Embassy and was later received by Monsieur Corbin who, grateful for my offer to help, passed me on to the *Médecin Chef*, in charge of all the English hospitals in which French wounded were to be found. He gave me permits to visit eight hospitals in my brother's county, with a special recommendation from himself. Armed with these, I almost skipped out of the Embassy and on to my home-bound bus.

The authorities who had refused me admittance proved to be glad of my official permit, which allowed, nay, asked, me to help their French patients, while absolving them from all responsibility with regard to the feelings of the local ladies.

I felt a great *serrement du cœur* as I entered a ward and saw Latin faces light up with hope and interest as they heard my first " *Comment ça va ?* " and when I told them that I had but just arrived from France, the convalescent crowded round me to hear my news of their beloved country. Walking from bed to bed I heard pitiful stories. They were all dying of homesickness because they had had no letters from their people ; no French newspapers to read. Their beds were littered with ' Daily Mirrors ' and ' Daily Sketches ' and English illustrated weeklies sent in from the wards of the English soldiers ; looked at languidly and then thrown irritably aside because the letterpress was unintelligible. Now they were opened again, and I was asked to name pictured towns and to translate what was written under the photographs. One boy asked me if I would write to him and, when I told him that I was often coming to see him now, he looked up at me wistfully and said, " *Quand-même !* " He wanted a letter all the same, a letter, stamped, and coming through the official postal source. It would make him feel less lost and lonely if a real letter was brought to him. I resolved to ask my eldest niece to write to him in French.

A letter from a *demoiselle Anglaise* would give
him a real thrill, poor boy.

They told me that everyone was very kind
to them, but they (of course) complained of
the *courants d'air* in the ward. Everyone of
French nationality seems to be terrified of
draughts of fresh air, and in English hospitals,
especially in warm June weather, windows and
doors are left permanently open. The *poilus*
also missed their wine, and grimaced ruefully
as they spoke of the drinks of water, milk,
tea, and barley water given to them.

" And we, who make our own wine in France !
What a shame that we can't get over a *tonneau*
or two," I lamented amid laughter. Then I
had to tell them all about my home in the
Midi.

One man was gloomily trying to wade through
a heavy volume of Châteaubriand. On the
table by his side were selected works of Corneille,
Racine, Lamartine, lent by a local lady. Not
even Victor Hugo, who might have had power
to move him ; Alexandre Dumas to thrill him ;
or Molière perhaps, to make him laugh. What
he was longing for was the popular ' weeklies '
of the *poilu*, ' *MATCH*,' ' *L'ILLUSTRATION*,' and
so on. By this time I had learned the tastes
of the French soldier, and knew that I must
immediately make another journey to London
to ransack the French book-shops and Con-
tinental book-stalls for light literature. I
promised to do this when I saw poor Châteaubriand tossed aside with a pettish " *Je n'y*

comprends rien." I consoled his reader by
saying that no one with a severe head wound
would be able to cope with classics, and that
many people with normal heads never could
read serious literature.

Four men, wrapped in dressing-gowns, were
seated around a table playing cards, while others
leaned over them watching their play with
interest.

" Le Belote, naturellement," I remarked.
Teeth gleamed instantly in dark intent faces,
and the man behind whom I stood showed me
his bad cards with a resigned shrug of the
shoulders. *" Pas de chance ! "* I said as I
moved away.

I left that ward warmed and comforted by
the instant acceptance as a friend who understood them by these pathetic French soldiers
stranded on our shores ; by their cordial fare-
wells and eager prayers that I should come
back to them soon. But, most of all, because
I could still work for the French Army—in
England. It was so extraordinary to find its
soldiers here. But for the magnificent disaster
of Dunkerque they would never have left
France.

The next day I went up to London and
searched for French newspapers, magazines,
and books, but met with scant success. The
latest *' MATCH '* was over a fortnight old, and
I could only find six sheets. I was offered
tattered copies of *' LA VIE PARISIENNE,'* published in 1937, for 1s. 9d. per copy.

Monstrous profiteering ; and in France we had never provided our *foyers* with this nudist periodical. But, haunted by those wistful faces in the hospital and remembering my promise to bring the men something in French to read, I weakly paid this exorbitant price and carried off a pile of these papers, resolving to wrap up the parcel and give it to some doctor or male visitor to present to the ward. In half an hour I had spent over £5 and had only enough magazines and books to supply *one* ward of *one* hospital, and there were eight hospitals to visit.

I had luncheon with an old friend in his comfortable Club—BEEF, of course, delicious pink beef, and apple pie and cream was my choice. I had been starved of English food for so long that, for the moment, I shunned any dish with a French or Italian name.

My host spoke of that glory of achievement, the evacuation of Dunkerque. A friend of his —in a high official position—had been unable to resist escaping secretly from his London duties and doing a little rescue work, and he had described the gallant flotilla of pleasure-steamers, private yachts, motor - launches, dinghies, tugs, which had rushed off to help get our men out of France. He had passed one tiny motor-boat, chugging slowly and doggedly along, its only occupant an old, old man with his white hair blowing in the breeze, holding grimly on to the steering-wheel. Blue-jackets chaffed him affectionately as they passed him, but he only looked up at them and shouted defiantly : " I'll GET there ! "

Of such is the Kingdom of Britain.

My French soldiers were thrilled with their magazines, stale as they were, and the idea came to me that since there must be so many French journalists now in London, it would surely be possible to print some small daily, or weekly, news-sheet for the soldiers. I must go up to London once more, visit friends in the English newspaper world, perhaps see the French Ambassador again, and find out what could be done.

The owner of the quarantine kennels where my Blackness was imprisoned had begged me not to visit Dominie for, at least, a week, so that he might have time to settle down in his new quarters and learn to have confidence in those who cared for him. Knowing his nervous temperament, I bore this separation for eighteen days, reassuring myself as to his welfare by telephone. It was very difficult to keep away. I was so much afraid that he would think himself deserted in a very strange world. Then, at last, I arranged to drive over to visit more French soldiers in the big hospital situated a few miles from the kennels, having first had luncheon with the Blackness.

I was almost frightened by his frantic joy when I appeared. He screamed, he waltzed, he tore madly round and round his grass run, making great leaps at me as he passed, one of them so high that, tall as I am, he grazed the bridge of my nose with his teeth, and the kennel-man had to mop me up with cotton wool soaked in peroxide to stop the bleeding. This calmed the Blackness, who can never bear to know anyone in pain, mental or bodily, and when I was staunched and we were alone together, we sat side by side on the grass as close to each other as we could get, and I combed his lovely ears and he kissed mine. Then, from a small tin pot we shared a meal. Before I left I promised him faithfully that I would find him a little house somewhere in a wood where he could run wild with me and hunt rabbits when he was free again and we should be, henceforth, always together. Then came the moment of betrayal. A favourite charcoal biscuit thrown to the farthest end of the run, and, while a small black Cocker rushed away to retrieve it, a door behind him swiftly and silently opened—and shut.

"Go to him, PLEASE," I said to the kennel-man as I ran down the path holding my hands over my ears.

The French soldiers in the new hospital gave me a great welcome. One or two of them came from the Midi, but most of them from Northern France. I heard the same story. No letters. No news from France. "*Nous languissons, vous savez.*" They must have their newspaper soon. They must have something. But I could still make them laugh, thank God.

The next day I went up to London once

more and interviewed several people in authority who all agreed that something must—and should very soon—be printed for the *poilus;* but the war news from France was so bad at the moment that perhaps it was just as well that wounded men could not read it. The Germans were advancing on Paris, but Reynaud had declared in an impassioned speech that the French would defend every lamp-post of their capital. Still, the lying propaganda of the Germans, their dive-bombing tactics and the machine-gunning of streets filled with refugees, their massed tanks crashing through and over every obstacle, even banks of dead and wounded bodies, was causing panic and despair in France.

Outside my Club I met an officer of the Grenadiers connected to John's family by marriage. He suddenly said to me—

" Tell me, Peggy, are the French going to conk on us ? "

" What do you mean—' conk on us ' ? " I asked him, unable to believe my ears.

" Collapse. Chuck. Leave us in the lurch," he answered.

Then I blazed. How dared he say such a thing, to me of all people ? I had worked with the French Army since the beginning of the war. They were magnificent men. They would fight to the last man. They were mad keen and so proud to be allied with us.

" Well—where is the French Army ? " he asked me sardonically.

" *Where is it ?* There are thousands of

French soldiers fighting like tigers at this moment, lacking ammunition, cut off by treachery, mashed into pulp by tanks, crowding the hospitals, manning forts in the Maginot Line and on the Italian frontier—in Syria. *Oh*, that you could ask such a question or imply anything so monstrous as that they would lay down their arms ! *I know them*— and I'd stake my life on the French Army." This, from me, shaken with passion.

"Well I'm glad to hear you say so—but personally I don't like the look of things," he said as I turned away.

For the rest of the day I was perfectly miserable. I longed for *Mademoiselle*. To tell her of this insult to our wonderful French Army and to see her great eyes light up with rage. I thought of our dear three-star General ; of those fine men it had been our privilege to meet at the moment of General Mobilisation, of the magnificent men of the Alpine Army, of their love and admiration for their English allies, how they scrambled for the little knots of red, white, and blue English ribbon we put in our *foyers* mixed with tiny *tricolor* cockades. "Conk on us ! "—" Leave us in the lurch ! " Those men !

Instinctively I walked straight to South Street, where, seated in a large cool room filled with great comfortable chairs and much-loved books, I should find a woman who, having suffered much herself, having conquered pain and loneliness, now spent a selfless life giving help and inspiration to others. A beautiful woman with a wonderful mind, the confidante of the best brains in London ; the originator of many charitable schemes, herself keeping always in the background. Only with her could I find calm and comfort. She would understand.

Mercifully she was there. She gave me what I sought. An hour of her company and conversation restored my balance and inspired me with fresh hope and new ideas. Talking together, we evolved a scheme to help the French. A gesture from Great Britain, made towards France, in this hour of her need, just to show her that we were with her in sympathy, sharing her agony and anxiety, would hearten the French people at this critical moment of their history. It must be a national gesture, and the help and collaboration of the Archbishop of Canterbury and of the French Ambassador, Monsieur Corbin, must be assured. I must seek interviews with them both at once, put forward my plan, and strive to persuade them to adopt it.

From that cool room I telephoned to Lambeth Palace and begged for an appointment, which was given for noon of the next day. I had made one with the French Ambassador, who was to see me in the afternoon about the work I was already doing for the French wounded soldiers in England, so that this promised well. If the Archbishop approved my scheme, he might allow me to propound it, giving the promise of his support, to Monsieur Corbin.

A kiss of benediction from the lady with the brave eyes, and, lighter of heart, I went out into the night.

Indeed I did! This was my first experience of a blacked-out London, and it certainly was very complete. Having much business to transact in London, I had arranged to stay the night in my Club, not ten minutes' distant from the block of flats that I had just left. In other days I had known my Mayfair by heart, but huge modern buildings had in many places now replaced the ancient houses that were familiar to me, and, anyhow, in this obscurity it was impossible to discern even outlines until one was within a yard of them. I had been warned of the utter bewilderment which might ensue upon stepping out from a brilliantly-lit hall into the total blackness which enfolds one as the front door is hurriedly shut behind one's back ; but, never having experienced it myself, I suppose I had not believed it possible that I could lose my bearings— which is exactly what I very soon did. Having groped my way down the front steps, stumbling at the bottom as I put forth a firm foot for the next step and jarred upon the pavement, I peered around me for a moment and then, guided by area railings, started feeling my way along. Another jar warned me that the pavement ceased at the entrance to a mews, which must be crossed. I crossed it and regained

pavement, and, after following it awhile, realised
that soon I must traverse the main street and
search for a turning on the left of it. I found
a turning, but of course it was the wrong turning,
and the name of the street, written above my
head, was invisible in that impenetrable gloom.
My electric torch was sitting cosily by my bed
in the Club, for, when I started out after
luncheon, I had intended to get back long
before the black-out. Lost as I was now, I
still could not regret the impulse that had
led me to the one woman in London who always
understood, but I learned the useful lesson
never, on any occasion, by day or night, to
go out without an electric torch in a war-time
England. Still it was both maddening and
humiliating to walk and walk and walk, meeting
no one, in search of a place which could not
be more than a few streets away.

Just as I was growing desperate, I almost
collided with a massive figure wearing the
King's uniform. I addressed it piteously and
asked if it could direct me to the Square where
I would be. It answered me very kindly, but
informed me that it was a stranger in those
parts, paying its first leave-visit to London.
Nevertheless, it chivalrously offered to help
find me before it found itself. So we groped
our way forward together, in search of trees,
the blind leading the blind with very little
success. Up streets and down streets we paced
uselessly, until suddenly my companion halted
with a suppressed oath.

"What is it ? " I inquired with solicitude.
" Did you ' stub your toe,' as they say ? "

" I've left my gas-mask at the house where
I was dining," he replied. " I did that last
week and I've only just been issued another—
I positively daren't ask for a third. I must
go back and find it. Do you think you could
direct me to the place where you picked me
up ? "

I began to laugh helplessly, the question was
so quaintly expressed—the answer so obvious.

" Since neither of us have the faintest idea
where we are now, I fear I can't promise to
do that. But why not ring a front door bell,
explain your predicament, and ask if you may
telephone to your friends ? " I suggested.

" Well—you see they aren't exactly friends—
in fact I don't even know their name and
address. They were friends of friends of mine
who just took me along in their car. I never
gathered who they were nor where they lived."

" As Mr Bennett said, ' It seems to me a
hopeless business,' " I replied. " Such a problem
must be solved by a man's brain."

" Well, if I walk about all night I may
recognise that house towards morning," he said
valiantly, " but I mustn't trouble you to do
that."

" I think, under the circumstances, we had
better try to find ourselves separately," I
agreed. " Very many thanks for your chivalrous
intent. Good-night and good luck ! "

Some time later, ghostly trees loomed before

me. I had found my Square and soon afterwards I found my Club. I wondered as, before getting into bed I made preparations for exit in case of an air-raid, placed precautionary overcoat, Alpine boots, and finally my gas-mask in readiness, whether that other lost soul ever found his.

Next morning in a vast and beautiful room in Lambeth Palace, overlooking green lawns bordered with roses and shaded by trees, I was received very courteously and kindly by a tired Archbishop. I had bombed myself into his study by my urgent telephone message which I knew would have had no effect had it not come from the wife of a man known, respected, and admired by the over-worked man before me. Having gained his presence I must now justify my entrance, and, as I saw the weariness in his face and heard it in the tones of his voice, I was almost overcome by nervous compunction. Then the memory of those fine men of the French Army for whom, and with whom, *Mademoiselle* and I had been so proud to work since the beginning of the war, flashed before my eyes and blinded them to aught else. I began to plead for them and for their beloved country, seeing only the horrible vision of their present agony.

And as the Archbishop listened he was moved to compassion, for he, also, loves France. He consented, if the collaboration of the French Ambassador could be assured, to help my scheme, but not in the impulsive headlong way I had tried to persuade him to use. Being

a man of the world and a diplomat, as well
as a man of God, he saw difficulties I had not
foreseen and the need of preparation and pause.
But as I left him he gave me his permission to
tell Monsieur Corbin that he would call in
person at the Embassy on Monday. As I
thanked him from my heart and turned to say
farewell, I remarked upon the beauty of his
green lawns, and I shall ever have a picture
of him silhouetted against that stretch of
verdure beyond the great window as he looked
wistfully out of it and said—

"Ah! I wonder if I shall be allowed to keep
my garden?"

In the Embassy that afternoon was an un-
accountably electric atmosphere—a continual
va-et-vient of French officers and civilians, grave-
faced, silent; messengers rushing from room
to room, telephone bells shrilling within them
as I waited to be received by the Ambassador.

Within his room I felt the same tense atmosphere—was it of impending danger? What
was it? He was sitting idly at his desk, and
at first I only saw his shadowed profile, but
when he turned I saw that his face was a ghastly,
tragic mask, drained of all colour. I poured
forth my project, but, unlike the Archbishop,
he who should have listened eagerly to my
plan to help France, gazed at me in heavy
silence, seeming quite unmoved, uttering no
comments until my tongue faltered and failed.

"Paris has fallen. It is too late, *chère
Madame*," he said quietly. "No one, now,

213

can save France from her fate. We need guns, and tanks, and aeroplanes, and munitions, not in a month's time, or even to-morrow, but now, now, NOW, at this very moment!"

I was stunned. Paris given up to the Germans! But Paul Reynaud had said that every lamp-post of Paris should be defended! I could not speak.

"So you see your warm-hearted scheme comes too late, *Madame*. Nevertheless I thank you, for France and all my countrymen, for what you have already done—and hoped to do—for our unhappy soldiers—who are being defeated by overwhelming numbers, crushed by tanks, machine-gunned from aeroplanes, as we speak." He covered his face with his hands.

I do not know what I said after that. But, in parting, once again I offered myself to the service of France should I be needed—if in any way I could help.

"Your services will be needed sooner than you know," I was quietly assured. I left the room and went out into the sunlit street, but, for me, the face of the sun was darkened.

Back in Hertfordshire once more, I scanned newspapers and listened to both English and French news feverishly. The situation in France was going from bad to worse and the news that Laval was again in power filled me with apprehension. For years we English in France had heard no good of Laval, and knew with what distrust and dislike he was regarded in

France. An ambitious, selfish and unscrupulous man, often described as a snake. Only self-advancement and self-interest would prompt any suggestions that he might make, never love of his country and anxiety for her welfare. I feared treachery.

Then came the incredible rumour of an Armistice, but this I still refused to believe. One evening, after tea, my brother, at last free from his manifold parochial duties, suggested that he and I should pay a visit to the neighbouring hospital, he to talk to the wounded English soldiers and I to my French. Accordingly we drove across a lovely common, amid heather and bracken, and into the beautiful park where the hospital is situated. The sinking sun cast long low shadows through the leaves of grand old beech trees, and the long approach was bordered to a depth of fifteen feet with blossoming willow-herb, as though a giant's paint-brush had splashed glowing stripes of purple-pink. Rabbits scuttled across the drive. Here and there a convalescent soldier lazed on the grass with visiting relatives. It was all so peaceful, and so English, and seemed so safe. I thought of France with the victorious invader desecrating her loveliness and shattering her peace. We, in our sea-girt island, had never known that horror since 1066. No wonder that few English people could understand the panic of the French peasants as hordes of German tanks, and pursuing aeroplanes, crashed through their villages and machine-gunned their old and infirm, their women and their children.

Should England be invaded in like manner, would those same German methods of ruthlessness and brute force have power to shake her people ? I thought not. I remembered the criticism of the Historian of the British Army. Comparing the French soldier with the English, he said—

" The French soldier follows strictly the military text-book. If he is surrounded by the enemy he will say : ' By all the rules of warfare I am defeated,' and will lay down his arms. The English soldier, in like position, will fight on desperately and refuse to acknowledge that he is beaten. Through sheer dogged cussedness he may, and often has, turned a technical defeat into a victory."

Just a difference of temperament and character. I felt very sure that if Germans succeeded in entering England, even the women would rush forth armed with brooms and frying-pans to defend their island.

Outside my first ward of French wounded I found a cluster of convalescents talking excitedly. Immediately they hobbled up to me and said that a rumour had been circulated that France had made—or would make—an Armistice with Germany.

" *Mais ce n'est pas vrai, Madame? C'est de la blague ? C'est de la mauvaise propagande Allemande, ça,—pour nous decourager.*"

I agreed that it could only be Fifth Column

lies further to discourage the already disheartened ; and I went into the ward.

Here, I was met with the same anxious questions from patients in the beds, but I soon turned the subject to the projected French newspaper. In a few days they would have it. Some of the best French journalists and at least one famous editor, escaped from Paris, were now in London and would set to work at once. This was good news and all faces lit up.

Then the voice of one of the B.B.C. Announcers rang down the room. A nurse had turned on the wireless so that the sprinkling of English soldiers in the ward might hear the six o'clock news. I stopped talking and sat down between the beds of two Frenchmen. My brother and I had forgotten that the six o'clock news in English would inevitably interrupt our talks with soldiers if we visited the hospital so late. What a bore, when there were so many Frenchmen who wanted letters from English maidens, and English newspapers translated for them ! Idly irritated by our stupidity, I resigned myself to wait, when I was abruptly shocked into rigidity by what the Announcer was saying. He was translating a speech made by Marshal Petain to the French people. France was overwhelmed by superior force. The French Army were to lay down their arms. An Armistice was to be signed with Germany. . . .

I suppose that only a superhuman could

hide all sign of a sudden and awful shock. I became aware of the intent stare of many pairs of dark eyes fixed upon my face, trying to read there the meaning of words they could not understand. With one of the greatest efforts of my life I made my face into an expressionless mask and relaxed my attitude, looking down upon the ground as though I were bored and only waiting for the Announcer's voice to cease.

When it did, I was assailed by a chorus of French voices asking me what had been said. They had heard the name of Marshal Petain mentioned. Of course he had contradicted that base rumour of an Armistice ?

Remembering how many of the men had bad head wounds, casually I shrugged my shoulders, answering vaguely and with some truth: "*Il n'y a rien de décidé encore.*" (Italy had not yet stated her terms. The jackal had not yet howled for his scraps of juicy meat.)

But one *poilu*, with a leg horribly wounded at Dunkerque, gave me a swift searching stare of disbelief. He must have seen some look of horror in my eyes before I could summon strength to veil them. Throwing off the bedclothes, he rolled himself out of bed, crawled to the wireless set, and turned it on to a French station. Then those sons of France, maimed in her service, heard the news of her dishonour from Petain's own lips.

Till I die I can never forget the scene that

followed. Those who had strength to rise from their beds got up, searched for their tunics, and tore off their decorations. The badly wounded drew the sheets over their heads. I tried to talk to these huddled heaps, but all that I could hear was "*J'ai honte! J'ai honte*," or deep muffled sobs. The convalescent soldiers clad in pyjamas and dressing-gowns at once formed a little battalion and prayed the Sister to let them go at once to join the English—to wipe out this shame.

But I wish I could forget the picture of one man of them all. Propped nearly upright by pillows, his shattered body held rigid by sand-bags, his head bandaged to cover the loss of an eye, this helpless figure could make no movement of anger or despair, but, from the one remaining eye, rolled great slow tears. . . .

When I thought of him in the watches of the night, symbol of my beloved France, maimed, conquered, dishonoured and heartbroken, my tears flowed too, and, in the morning, I almost felt surprise that they had not stained my pillow red.

CHAPTER XXIII.

SHADOWED DAYS.

SHADOWED days filled with a great anxiety and unrest. Would Germany take over the whole of France? In this case the English who had stayed out there would be trapped and herded into concentration camps, if they found it impossible to escape into Spain during the space of time which must elapse while the terms of Armistice were being discussed. The English lady who had taken refuge in my little 'Sunset House' would doubtless flee—if she had not already flown. *Mademoiselle* of the *Château* below me—what would she do now that her gallant work for the French Army was rendered null and void? Our *Foyers des Soldats de France*, which she had founded in the High Alps, had, at anyrate, comforted the French Alpine Army while they watched in lonely frontier forts and desolate snow-bound villages. Now they would be filled with Italian soldiery.

The work to which we had given so much love and energy was over, and I knew that *Mademoiselle* must be hiding an almost broken heart alone in her dim old *Château*. American born, she had been naturalised French eighteen years ago. Would she now take up again her American nationality ? Then she would find escape easier. And those other English friends, some of them too poor to contemplate life in England with its crushing taxation ? In France, the rate of exchange had enabled them to live, simply, without cares. Some of them, I knew, could not possibly afford the expensive fare home, and, in any case, since the war all the English in France had been money-rationed, so that even the very rich had to curtail staff and expenditure and had never enough to lay aside ready for a possible emergency.

Once again my mind was turning round and round the same sad subject, like a wild squirrel in a cage trying ever to find escape and finding none. My visits to the wounded French soldiers added only to my unhappiness, for theirs was so great. All were in terror for their families, now at the mercy of the Nazis—if they were not already dead. No letters or news from France had been received by any of the men. Most of them came from Northern France, which had long since been swept over and devastated by German tanks and aeroplanes. Where, now, were their women and their children ? Alive or dead ? All lost——

What could one say to these tragic soldiers whose past, present, and future was all horror ? When the news of the Armistice came, in some hospitals the English private soldiers had shown their indignation against France for deserting her Ally—" putting us in the cart," " landing us in the soup," " doing the dirty on us "— and they were unable to understand the Frenchmen's reiterated cry, " *Nous sommes vendus !* "

Here there was work to be done—I could tell the English about the magnificent men of the French Army that I had known—of their love of the English and their pride in our alliance. I could explain that anguished cry of the French soldiers in the ward. Indeed they *had* been sold to the Germans by treacherous politicians. And, later, I could hearten my Frenchmen with the news that a French General in London, called de Gaulle, was forming a Free French Army of loyal refugees and any Frenchmen who could still escape to serve with him under the tricolor. Very soon they heard the voice of this General de Gaulle on the wireless, like a bugle calling every free Frenchman to come and join him. This was at least a gallant gesture, and it heartened me too.

But I had the wild longing of a hurt animal to find some secret place in which to hide and lick my wounds. The effort to be gay with my brother's care-free children was too great. I feared that the moment would come when overstrained nerves could not be longer restrained, and that I might cease to be able to disguise my irritability and unrest. They were so full of joyous vitality, those children, that I dreaded clouding their happiness with my own grief, or to shock them into hurt surprise by my irritability. Better far to leave my brother's lovely old Rectory in which I had been so lovingly welcomed home, before that could happen. I must find a small cottage, somewhere near woods, where Dominie, my little Blackness, could run wild and hunt rabbits when he was loosed from the quarantine kennels, and where, if my troubled mind would let me, I could write. Such a cottage might not easily be found, but that it would be found for me, of that I was sure.

In the meanwhile I must occupy every moment of my time. I must distract my thoughts. How better than by furnishing that dream-cottage that would one day be mine? The August sales were opening in London. I would profit, now, by the reduced prices of everything necessary for a small home before the Purchase Tax came into being. Everything could be stored until I found my cottage.

I told no one of this decision, knowing that everyone would think me raving mad to buy furniture for a house that only existed in my imagination. More book-royalties had come in, so that modest expenditure was justified. I made lists of necessities and went up to London as often as I could for orgies of shopping.

I have never enjoyed shopping so much since those enchanted days when I bought my *trousseau*. Then, for the first time in my life I could be wildly extravagant, for my ' Fairy Godmother ' had given me a cheque for a hundred pounds as her wedding present and my husband-to-be another with which to buy linen. Now, my position was even more interesting and enviable, for having lost everything in France, I must be careful of every penny and plan and plot and scrape so that my cottage could, nevertheless, be well - equipped and charming.

I explained all this to the shop-assistants in every store and department that I visited, threw myself upon their mercy, and begged their kind help. They all responded to my appeal and drew forth ancient pre-war stock at reduced prices, but of wonderful quality, and in some cases they reminded me of small, necessary things I had forgotten to include on my lists. I described the home I hoped to have, and, though much amused that I was furnishing a dream-cottage, they realised the wisdom of it, since every day prices were rising and stock getting scarcer. All the shops with whom I dealt consented to store my purchases until I wanted them, but all urged me to find my new home as quickly as possible before Germany started bombing London, when my goods would be in danger ; or Hitler tried invasion, when all transport would be stopped. Every day more men were being called up. At the moment my furniture, &c., could be delivered to me by the store where I bought it, if my home were within a certain radius of London, but later——

I promised swiftly to find a house for my furniture and left the Manager laughing.

Because the house would be in the woods, everything inside it should be green, so that on entering one felt that it was but a continuation of the forest. I chose a carpet of a tender shade of almond green, little divan-beds covered in green; blankets and sheets, also green; and a chintz for curtains and covers to match the carpet, with a design of buff and russet leaves; the oak, ash, beech, lime and elm of England and, by an extraordinary chance, the vine and loquat of Provence. These sprays of pale leaves toned beautifully with the cheap unvarnished oak furniture, simple and solid, which I chose for all my rooms. There would surely be three bedrooms in my cottage—mine, a spare room, and a maid's room—also a bathroom, living-room, and kitchen. I bought furniture for these and then had a glorious time equipping the perfect and practical kitchen with utensils and gadgets. This planning for something permanent in a strange and shifting world was salutary for the soul; and on these selfish shopping days in London I combined work for others.

I had written to the National Institute for the Blind, who, two years before, had asked my permission to make my first book, 'Perfume from Provence,' into a 'Talking Book' (gramophone records) for the blind. I had already, very joyfully, given my consent for all three of my books to be put into Braille and Moon type, feeling so proud that my writings might perhaps give a little light and laughter to those who sit in darkness. But not everyone can learn to read these types, particularly difficult for the illiterate private soldier, or the very old—and so the idea of the ' Talking Book ' was born that those who could not read might listen.

When I answered the Librarian's letter so long ago in France, I had told him how much I should love to read aloud my own book to the blind, and he replied that, if I would only do that, they would hold up its recording indefinitely—until I could come to England.

Well, here I was in England, and now seemed the perfect moment to start my readings. So I wrote to the Librarian apprising him of my arrival and asking when he would like me to come up to London to see him.

He made an appointment for a voice-test for the following week. Apparently a voice-test is always necessary even for voices professionally trained as mine was. On a gramophone record a melodious voice may sound harsh, and, vice versa, a clear voice, indistinct—something to do with the spacing between the lines of the record, I believe. It was explained to me later, but I am not mechanically-minded and all that I took in was that very large discs must be used for Talking Books and the lines placed very close together to save quantity and expense, and this closeness affects the sound produced.

As yet I had no car of my own, but I felt

the lack of my '*Désirée*' less because an excellent bus and coach service passed the Rectory gate and I could leap on to a Green Line coach at any hour of the day and be conveyed direct to London. Cross-country journeys, made in this way, were exhausting, for connections had become bad.

But I enjoyed those rides. The coaches were so comfortable and the conductors so civil; even when a passenger struggled in with an illegitimate amount of week-end suit-cases, they winked the other eye and were always kind and helpful. Human nature always thrills me, and I had unlimited opportunities to study it during those journeys; rich (being unable to get petrol for their cars) and poor, sometimes of many nationalities, mixed together, all carrying gas-masks; all telling each other of their novel war-experiences, adventures, and escapes, and confronting their difficulties with the same high heart and humour. They were cosy, those journeys, because everyone was so neighbourly and kind. The cold English reserve and dislike of being herded together had vanished. Company gave courage, and the knowledge that we were all 'in for it,' sooner or later, and shared the same dangers, gave comradeship.

If I had not travelled in that coach I should never have overheard this remark, made by a fat comfortable woman behind me—

" You know I can't get that Lady Fortescue off me 'eart. 'Er and 'er little Sunshine 'Ouse.

Wot d'yer suppose 'as 'appened to 'er now the French 'ave gone and done this awful thing ? 'Ow, I *do* 'ope she's orlright."

Only intense shyness and a dread of making myself conspicuous in that crowded coach refrained me from taking out my regulation identity card and holding it out over the back of my seat to reassure that kind woman. The little episode was somewhat startling, but very comforting somehow.

The Talking Studio is in St Dunstan's, and so, as the day was fine, I decided to walk to it across Regent's Park. I chose the longest way round so as to peer into the war-time Zoo and wave to such animals who had not been evacuated to the safer area of Whipsnade. Outside the gates the car-park was empty save for one solitary taxi ; and inside them all seemed strangely quiet too. An uncomfortable thought swam into my mind—supposing, when the long-expected air attacks started on London—that a bomb shattered the confining bars of—say—the lions' cages, or broke down the walls of the snake house ? Rather exciting for the occupants of houses in Regent's Park. I had a vision of a staid butler entering a dining-room to announce, in that voice which only changing tradition and not a mere war accident could shake—

" Excuse me, sir, but I think it is my duty to inform you that there is a cobra in the kitchen. Cook is naturally a little upset. Having no suitable weapon to deal with the situation personally, should I telephone to the Police, or to the Home Guard ? "

Or—

" Excuse me, My Lord, but hearing an irregular sound outside, I opened the front door to reassure myself that all was in order, and I regret to inform Your Lordship that a large lion bounded into the hall and is now at large. Your guns have just been returned from the gunsmith's ready for Your Lordship's week-end shoot in Suffolk. May I be permitted to fetch Your Lordship's gun-case and ammunition from the dressing-room ? I can gain access to it by—hem—the back stairs."

Next day—

BIG GAME SHOOTING IN REGENT'S PARK. LORD X. BAGS LARGE LION.

No such newspaper heading could startle us in these fantastic days.

I was very charmingly received in the Talking Studio by the Librarian, who was chatting with a grave-eyed side-whiskered man, introduced to me as Joseph Macleod, the well-known B.B.C. Announcer. Of course I recognised the tones of that familiar voice the moment he spoke to me. The Librarian told me that most of the Talking Books were read for recording by the Announcers of the B.B.C., who gladly gave their free time for so good a cause. I confessed that this new ordeal terrified me, but Mr Macleod assured me that for his part, he loved his readings : " Very soon you will find yourself unable to keep away from the

Studio," he affirmed positively. " I find it like a drug, the more I take of it the more I find I want it."

When he had gone, the Librarian put me into an armchair in a little sound-proof room with a silver ball swinging before me (the microphone) and a table with a red and a green electric bulb before me and an electric bell-button close at hand. I was told that when the recording was about to begin the red light would gleam. After this, every sound made in that room would be registered, so that if I wanted to sneeze or cough I must instantly ring the bell at my side to warn the Librarian to stop recording, else the record would be spoiled—unless, of course, a sneeze or cough were recorded in the text. A green light would signal the end of the record and then I should be permitted to indulge in any paroxysm I pleased.

The moment that I was shut in alone and the red light gleamed after a nerve-racking pause, I felt a nervous tickling in my throat and nose, but I conquered it and only hoped that the silly quick-beating of my heart could not be heard by that sensitive disc in the adjoining Studio. I had first to announce the name of the book and its author, and then the fact that Winifred Fortescue was reading it. I longed to say " and she's perfectly terrified because she's never done this before." That would have excused any mistakes I might make.

When the record was finished and I con-

fided my impulse to the Librarian, he exclaimed :
" Oh ! I *wish* you had ! Your listeners would
have loved it. It would have sounded so
natural."

Sticky with fright, I was refreshed with a
delicious cup of tea. The ordeal was over,
and the record I had made would be listened
to by the committee, who would then decide
whether my voice was suitable for recording
purposes.

A few days later, a letter from the Librarian
told me that I had passed my voice-test honour-
ably and the Committee would be very grateful
if I would read my book for the benefit of the
blind. Other appointments were arranged, and
thenceforth I went up to London fairly regularly.
Mr Macleod proved to be a false prophet where
I was concerned, for I never mastered my
nervousness and had to fight a·kind of mental
paralysis which I felt stealing over me towards
the end of each record. For the red warning
signal is flashed to tell the reader that he has
time to read only about half a page more before
the record is used up. He must therefore swiftly
select a good stopping-place, not too far off,
and leave himself time to pause for the fraction
of a second and then announce, " Continued
on the other side of this record," or, " End
of record one." There is always the risk of
spoiling the record by bad judgment of time,
but thank heaven I never did that, though I
daresay I made many mistakes while reading,
especially as the Librarian came into the little

sound-proof room at the beginning of my first sitting to say: "Lady Fortescue, do you think that you could translate any French sentences in your book as you go along? You see the majority of your readers won't be able to understand French." From that moment, whenever I saw a sentence in italics ahead of me, I broke into a cold sweat lest swift, colloquial translation failed me.

Then there was the day when, in the middle of a record, I heard a resounding hammering on metal from without. Feeling sure that this noise would ruin the record, for the first time I rang the bell to warn the Librarian that something untoward was happening. There was a long, long pause, but no one came near me, and then, suddenly, on went that red light and I knew that the Librarian had just given me time to cough or sneeze and was now recording again.

I finished reading to the accompaniment of that clanging noise, and when I emerged from my room asked him if it would have spoiled my record. He told me that it came from a building being constructed by the Office of Works, not from St Dunstan's premises, so that nothing could be done about it. "You can hear it faintly in the records," he said, "but not enough really to matter. Oddly enough the only time when that noise would have sounded very appropriate—when we were reading one of Jeffery Farnol's books about a blacksmith hammering on his anvil—there was complete silence next door!"

I had very nearly finished reading my book when, on writing to the Librarian to suggest an appointment, he answered that the Talking Studio had received a direct hit from a bomb and that he was still crawling about in the crater to see if he could salvage any of his records and machinery. When he had done scrabbling he would let me know the result.

CHAPTER XXIV.

DARKNESS AND LIGHT.

WHEN in London I often went to the Headquarters of the French Red Cross, and one day was taken to see their *Depôt* of clothing and comforts for French soldiers and refugees. Here were rooms filled with clothing of every description, from *layettes* for babies to voluminous petticoats for grandmothers, and the place was crowded with pathetic people of both sexes and all ages being outfitted from the collection by English, but French-speaking, volunteers. Down in the basement was installed a busy little French cobbler amid a huge pile of apparently derelict shoes and boots which, I was assured, he would repair *à merveille* for these poor refugees.

I talked to many of them and was informed that a complete family—parent tree, branches and twigs, not to mention uncles, aunts, and cousins ; forty-two souls in all—had managed to escape to England from Brittany in their own fishing-boat. Four ladies of the party were in an interesting condition, but *grandmère*, with French foresight, had also contrived to find and bring with them the family *sage-femme* to deliver the young Frenchmen safely in England.

I heard, too, from a woman who had escaped from Toulon that when the news of the Armistice came through, the whole town was in an uproar. The people rushed, raging, to the civic authorities who were so terrified of bloodshed that they announced that this was a false report. Whereupon scenes of hysterical joy were witnessed, citizens ringing the church bells and embracing soldiers and sailors, everyone shouting " *Ce n'est pas vrai ! Ce n'est pas vrai !* " But it *was* true.

Oh ! the tragedy of it all. . . .

The French Red Cross dared no longer send their ambulances, nor their supplies of bandages and medicaments over to France for the French wounded, knowing that they would certainly fall into German hands and never reach their destination. And one day when I went to see the *Médecin Chef* in his office, I found him with bowed head staring silently at visions of his own. He told me that the Germans were sending all the best French doctors and specialists to tend German wounded, and that he must go back at once to France.

" Madness ! " I cried. " They will send you, too."

He looked at me with tragic eyes and said that this must be risked. In his opinion it was the duty of every French doctor now in England to go back and try to help his wounded countrymen.

I thought of those pathetic *poilus* that *Mademoiselle* had nursed in the improvised *Infirmerie* she had made in her Studio at the outbreak of war. Those great children, so touchingly grateful for her care of their raw feet, cut and septic fingers, coughs and colds. Of the little *Postes de Secours* of the French Red Cross up in the High Alps which had lacked almost everything until we furnished them with ether, iodine, antiseptic lotions and dressings, *ventouses*, blankets and pillows. We had found one doctor applying boiled water to small wounds because he had nothing else and wished to keep the faith of his patients by innocent pretence. He nearly cried for joy when *Mademoiselle* unpacked her store of medicaments and bandages before his anxious eyes. The hospitals had been equipped, but the First Aid stations for men in the rear of the Army could not yet be supplied.

And now, when the rooms of the French Red Cross in London were piled up with comforts and medical necessities, these could not be sent to a France under Nazi rule, for they would never reach those maimed Frenchmen, and *Mademoiselle* and I could no longer help our *poilus*, who needed us so sorely. If this thought was bitter to me, what must it be to her, caged in her old *Château* in the South of France ? She would eat her heart out, alone there, scorched by the fierce August sun and the fiercer fire of her frustrated fighting spirit— a second Joan of Arc burned at a spiritual stake.

Now that her feverish activities to help the French Army were at an end, and, under happy conditions, her overstrained body might rest, her thoughts would give her no peace. The irony of it all.

I must find a little home for us all, somewhere, soon. *Mademoiselle* might be forced to flee from France, and I had news that our other dear neighbour was on her way back. Our British Vice-Consul in Cannes had succeeded in finding two cargo boats for the transport of British residents of the region. How many of my friends would travel home on these?

Those two cargo boats, now spoken of as the ' Hell Boats,' have been described only too vividly by Mr Somerset Maugham who travelled on one of them—the iron decks which became almost red-hot in the sun, the lack of sanitation, the scarcity of food and water, and the fortitude and good humour of the hapless British, of all ages and sexes, herded together like cattle upon them. I met him some time afterwards, a grey ghost of the man I had met at luncheon with the Phillips Oppenheims in France. He had had no real rest since his return from that awful voyage. At once he was asked to broadcast his experience, and, after that, his clever brain and pen were commandeered for work of national importance.

Suddenly her sister had a cable from my other dear neighbour in France, simply saying " Am here." The cable came from Gibraltar. The Hell Boats had come in—without her—

and we had been wondering anxiously what had become of her. One of the passengers on Hell Boat No. 1 told us that she was travelling on a small 150-ton yacht, *pronounced unseaworthy*, and this increased our anguish. Thereafter we had no news for two or three weeks, and then, at last, we heard that she had arrived in England and was safe with cousins in the South, and we breathed again.

She had had the most awful voyage. Unable to face the conditions of the Hell Boats, she had thankfully accepted a berth on this little private yacht, manned by a crew of amateurs likewise making their escape. The men managed the sailing and the women did the cooking—when they could stand up. But the weather was terrible. The yacht started with the two Hell Boats, which were convoyed only as far as Marseilles. Then they were ordered to proceed via Oran, and warned that the lightships, marking the passage in, would not be lit as we were at war. The sea was so tremendous that passengers on the Hell Boats gave the yacht up for lost, time and again, as she disappeared into the trough of the waves, but, almost miraculously, she weathered the storm. Outside Oran, her passengers were startled to see lights blazing from the lightships.

France must have signed an Armistice with Germany! She had. The English Admiral at Oran at once visited the French Admiral and found him sitting before a table sobbing, his head laid upon his folded arms, broken by this awful news. He could not believe in treachery, or a Nazi plot, and when the English Admiral assured him of this and said, "It's all right, your ships are here. You will just go on fighting with us," he repeated over and over again, "I can't. *Pétain* has given us these orders. *Pétain* . . ."

It was wonderful to see and talk with one who had shared the lovely cosy intimate life of our tiny village in the mountains and to hear of *Mademoiselle*, loved so much by us both. She had refused to leave her beloved France. She would stay and help the French until it became impossible. It was characteristic of her. But now I had someone with whom to share this constant anxiety for the welfare of *Mademoiselle*—someone to whom I could talk of our lovely life in Provence. . . .

CHAPTER XXV.

PARADISE — FOUND.

WHEN I awoke one morning, to my intense surprise I experienced that delightful sensation I had always felt on waking in my youth—a certainty that something both nice and exciting was going to happen to me during the day. Then, it was accompanied by a bubbling *joie-de-vivre* which effervesced until flattened by the last war. It was pleasant to feel again that stirring of expectation, and, having drunk my morning coffee, I began, with interest, to open my letters wondering what I might find therein. With a faint sense of disappointment, I found nothing of particular note within those envelopes, and, wondering if, for the first time in my life, my queer instinct had been deceived, I stretched for my copy of ' The Times.' As always, I turned to the Personal column, which is to me one of the most romantic things still left to us. Someone has a rocky island to sell in some remote sea—a yacht—a caravan. A young man offers himself for any post affording danger and adventure. An old Castello on the shores of the Adriatic is for sale—an orange grove in the Balearic Islands—or there may be some fantastic advertisement which leaves you guessing deliciously. To me that column is better far than a visit to a wonderful picture gallery, for each advertisement conjures up personal pictures of the imagination. I see that lonely island with sea birds wheeling over its rock-cliffs and great green waves dashing and thundering into its caves. There is a little safe sandy bay, perfectly private ; ideal for my bathing, and above it a turf-covered ledge of rock (facing south, of course) where I can lie, bare to the sun and wind, to dry. For of course, in imagination, I buy the island, I also buy the yacht, the caravan, the castle, and the orange grove ; and I engage the services of that daring young man to run them all for me and share the adventures I shall certainly have.

But to-day, although nothing thrilling or peculiar at once arrested my attention, yet that feeling of expectation persisted. Then God suddenly pointed a radiant finger to a quiet little three-line advertisement and I read—

" Week-end cottage, unfurnished, without electricity, wonderfully situated, hidden by woods, surrounded by streams. Low rent suitable tenant."

Perfect for Dominie and me. A little green secret place where, comforted by the companionship of trees and forest things, I could find courage to begin life yet again. There, I could write. And my Blackness, released from his concentration camp, could hunt rabbits, foxes, badgers.

I must get up and dress. I must answer that advertisement immediately, before some other snatched our cottage. But no! If it had not been meant for US, I should never have been shown that advertisement——

Still, as I answered it and asked for fuller particulars, I did hope that I might prove 'suitable' to the owner.

My letter was answered, by return of post, from the city of London. The typewritten reply was obviously dictated by a man of business, for on half a page of notepaper were tersely stated the few particulars I wanted to know. The signature, written in his own hand, was indecipherable. The cottage was on his private estate in Sussex. It had a right-of-way leading down to it through the woods, up which, in low gear, a small car could mount to the main road along which motor-coaches passed every hour to the railway station he recommended me to use. There was an excellent train service to London, and the journey took only forty-five minutes. If I cared to come down to see the cottage, would I please make an appointment for any day and time. The hours of departure of the motor-coaches meeting certain trains were enclosed, typed on a separate sheet. The coaches stopped at the gates of the main house where the key of the cottage might be had. I liked my future landlord already. He was honest, or he would not have stated the ' crab ' of the cottage (no electricity) in his advertisement, and only a man of imagination and literary sense could have worded that advertisement. A divine picture of peace painted in eight words. Having achieved this masterpiece, he wasted no more paint. His letter, curt and courteous, only spoke of practical details—and not many busy men would have troubled to look up the times of coaches which coincided with trains. He was thoughtful. I looked forward to meeting him.

Telling no one my secret, I arranged the day of my visit, justifying my journey by a visit to the French *Croix Rouge* as I crossed London. Feeling delightfully young and guilty, I hopped into my train and dreamed of woods and waters until I reached my destination, where a big green coach awaited me, as promised.

We drove through one of the most charming villages I have seen, with at least three perfect houses I should have been thrilled to own— half timbered, gabled, yellow-washed between the beams, roofed with moss-grown stone slabs, tangled with creepers. There was also a little lake bordered by green lawns running down from rose-covered cottages ; and then a straggling street with a tiny antique shop, its windows filled with really good things my practised eye could appreciate as we flashed past ; an ancient church ; an inn called ' The Bent Arms '—(all ready to enfold me). But this was not *my* village. I had been told that the bus journey would take me fifteen minutes and barely five had passed. Now, undulating wooded country, lovely country with, from every hill-top, a glorious open view stretching across the Downs to the coast, and then—the coach stopped before iron gates and the conductor told me that the great gabled red-tiled house within them was the place I sought. I got out with a quickening heart and stood looking vaguely about me. At which of these lodges and courtyards and doors should I present myself—in my shabby French uniform?

And then I saw, standing under an archway of shrubs, a white-clad lady. She advanced, smiling, towards me, asked me if I were myself, and then said, in a tone which graciously implied the very nicest things—

"I was reading your last book when you wrote to my son. I keep it by my bed."

This was warming, and I forgot my shyness.

She sent for the keys of my cottage and led me on to a wide terrace overlooking—OH !— OVERLOOKING !—— I had not believed that anything so wonderful could exist in England. Sloping lawns led down to a stairway cut in grey rocks, down, down, and down again. Far below lay a chain of lovely little lakes and waterfalls, rising one above the other up a glorious wooded valley. On one side of it were great cliffs of grey rock broken by shrubs and cypress trees. But this might be Provence ! On the other, above woods of great and glorious beech trees, beyond plantations of Scots firs cutting the sky-line, were rolling fields and wooded valleys world without end.

" Amen," I said to myself. So be it. This is to be my home.

We began to climb down those stone steps. Half-way down my White Lady suddenly stopped and, smiling to me, pointed her finger downwards. And far below us I saw the tops of chimneys rising up through a sea of foliage.

My cottage !

We reached the end of the steps, wound our way through a tunnel of rhododendrons, and reached a little wicket gate marked PRIVATE. Then we walked down a narrow path, slid down a slope of slippery turf, under a natural arch of nut trees pillared on either side by hollies, and there, beside a great rock, stood my cottage, a quaint little gabled redness with queer tall chimneys.

Before it stretched rough grass and, beyond that, the lowest and largest of the lakes. Old apple trees, with branches whiskered with lichen, hung over the water, upon which floated great white lotus lilies. Around the lakes were massed every kind of luxuriant flowering shrub and tree, planted in clumps, here and there, most beautifully. The first of the waterfalls cascaded down between them, and above it there was a glimpse of the second, shaded by a great oak tree, beyond that, a third—and a fourth—and a fifth ! At the head of each waterfall were great flat stepping-stones crossing the water where it narrowed at each lake's end. Grass paths edged them on either side, and, from their margin, the woods rose steeply until the eye was lost in the green gloom of giant beech trees and mysterious whispering firs.

Behind the cottage, bordered by a thicket of rhododendrons and azaleas, dashed a larger waterfall (MY waterfall) into a tiny stream—MY stream—which ran between steep grassy banks down MY valley, a secret inlet of rough grass shut in by trees and guarded by one graceful giant beech.

Everywhere I heard the sound of many waters. That would be the name of my new home, ' Many Waters.' . . .

My White Lady wandered tactfully away, letting her butler show me over the cottage. I must try, now, to be practical. But what did it matter what the house was like inside with all heaven outside it ?

Be practical! BE PRACTICAL! Can you live alone in so solitary a place, for will you ever find a maid who would stay there with you ? (I knew of one who would, but she was in Provence.) How will you ever get furniture, fuel, and supplies down here ? What about your car ? There is no garage and no road approach ; in case of illness, no telephone, and what doctor would slide down that precipice to come to your aid ? . . .

That is all you get for trying to be practical. A dreadful dunching depression. Red flags waving at you where you long to walk. Wise counsel when you are full of exciting folly. . . .

Then the cottage, having been abandoned to the jackdaws for so long, must surely be damp? But it was not. It was warm and dry as a bone, therefore solidly built. The butler showed me room after room, and then, very patiently, all over again. It had been re-decorated; the walls were distempered a golden cream colour, but, to live there comfortably, holes must be knocked in walls to make rooms communicate, and could I bear to walk through the kitchen to reach the only bath and throne-room? No, a thousand times, No! I must have my own bathroom upstairs. Money would have to be spent on that cottage to make it habitable for me, and, with a war on, was I justified in spending the little reserve I had?

Doubting Thomas is, to me, the least attractive of the disciples. Better far, with all his faults, the impulsive Peter. Nevertheless, I must try to emulate Thomas and not to be too Peterian. Thank goodness I need not make my decision now. I would go back to the sane atmosphere of my brother's Rectory and there balance pros and cons. And then I realised that all those 'cons' that had crawled into my mind were his inevitable questions when I confessed my project. I funked that confession.

"Would you like to see my little pigs? They are pink. And when one gives them spinach leaves they waggle their tails." This delightfully irrelevant suggestion came from my White Lady. Perfect. Pitch practicality and pessimism into the lake. Visit little pigs and make them waggle their tails. If I had had one, it would surely have waggled then from pure pleasure.

" And I have fifty babies." The White Lady pursued the conversation, between pants, as we climbed the mountain.

Nothing could surprise me any more. Nothing was real. This place could only be the figment of a dream, it was far too lovely to be true. Why not fifty babies since they must all be made of gossamer, or just heads and wings, if they lived here.

Then came enlightenment.

" We gave up our house to a kindergarten school evacuated from Deptford, and we live now in little lodges. One day you must see my babies. They came here so dirty and so pale and ill, and after a few weeks they bloom like the flowers. They are sweet."

A sudden squealing heard above us. The little pigs ? Or the babies ? Babies. No ! gnomes and elves trotting and tumbling down the steep grassy slope, red-capped, green-capped, blue-capped, yellow-capped, a medley of colour as though someone had suddenly spilled a basket of flowers upon those lawns and the wind was blowing roses, cornflowers, buttercups, and marigolds down upon us. The White Lady was pelted with them, entwined by them, very nearly garlanded with them as they climbed about her, and with difficulty extricated herself from the clinging of tiny hands ; stilling the clamour of fifty shrill piping voices with promises to visit their owners after tea. The gnomes and elves were then marshalled into a procession by their guardians and we continued our ascent.

The little pigs fulfilled the promise of the White Lady and dutifully waggled their tails as we fed them leaves of spinach—and, incidentally, with her son's latch-key which fell from a ridiculous little pocket, and, after fruitless search was found ten days later, wedged between the teeth of one of them, discovered by an end of string hanging from the corner of its mouth.

I climbed into my coach a little dizzily at the end of that day of enchantment.

It was during the small hours of the next morning that those 'cons' overwhelmed me. Oh! those small hours when the vitality is low and dreams are dead. I lay awake in my brother's great silent Rectory and my imagination was as empty as my stomach. Doubts and apprehensions assailed me and chilled my heart and feet. Shivering, I crept out of bed at last and drafted a polite and practical letter to be sent to him who would have been my landlord—a terribly sane and sensible letter, utterly false to my desires and my heart, entirely foreign to my style and self. Then, with a miserable sense that I had done the right thing in refusing the cottage and should regret it all my life, I crawled, like the worm I was, back into bed feeling as though I had been evicted a second time from a loved home.

CHAPTER XXVI.

THE LAUGHING LANDLORD.

I DO not know if my dullness of spirit during those two succeeding days was remarked by my family. In any case, I could have been but a depressing companion at that time, and so, perhaps, they did not notice an access of deadness in me. But on the morning of the third day I was jerked out of my apathy by surely the most extraordinary letter prospective landlord ever wrote to possible tenant. Mine regretted that I had decided not to take his cottage, and then, with astounding agility as it seemed to me, proceeded to leap over the mountainous obstacles I had raised, as though they were the primrose-clumps which carpeted his valleys. This he did, "not to make me change my mind, but from the theoretical point of view that I must be shown how all the difficulties I had mentioned could be solved."

Difficulties were catalogued numerically, each with its solution appended. There were seven of each. So far the letter was practical prose, but suddenly it soared to the level of Jules Verne. The succeeding paragraph fired my imagination as a lighted fuse fires a petrol bomb—

" I do, however, think that incidents are bound to occur in a place like my cottage, which is very secluded. For instance in the event of bad weather rain may pour down the right-of-way in torrential floods and make the use of even a small motor-car difficult. There is also the possibility of animals, such as pigs, having escaped from neighbouring farms and become wild, which are both unpleasant and dangerous to encounter (this has happened on the estate). The number of foxes is a menace, and vermin of all kinds are growing in numbers now that hunting is scarce and keepers even scarcer. Even lakes have to be looked after, and if left alone for any considerable time will produce snakes of unnatural dimensions.

" All these things have to be taken into account, and I am inclined to think that, especially in war-time, it would be better for the cottage to be occupied by a retired couple who would have time to organise everything, particularly their own protection."

There was a nice irrelevant postscript, reminiscent of his mother—

P.S. " I do not expect that I have heard the last about the pig swallowing my key. I hope we do not get fined by the Marketing Board for feeding pigs on scrap metal." . . .

O excellent young man !

I folded up that letter and put it in a very safe place. Then walked straight to the telephone, rang up the office of the writer, and made an arrangement to meet him next day at my Club in London.

A very large young man whose majesty of mien and manner was happily belied by very keen blue eyes which could surely be made to twinkle, kept the appointment. I handed him the first week's rent of the cottage, and those wary eyes widened. "What is this?" he asked suspiciously. "My first week's rent," I replied meekly.

"But—I thought that you had decided not to take the cottage?" he demurred in astonishment.

"Your letter reversed my decision," I retorted. "Your picturesque perils are not to be resisted. At anyrate life on your estate can never be dull."

Slowly the majesty melted, the blue eyes danced, the mouth curled into a mischievous smile, and suddenly I was talking, not to an alarming man of business, but (in spite of the disparity of years) to a kindred spirit.

And so, the bargain was concluded and 'Many Waters' was mine "for five years, or the duration of the war, whichever is the longer."

CHAPTER XXVII.

SOUTHWARD BOUND.

THAT evening I made my confession to my brother, who heard it with his customary sympathy and understanding, though with some sadness and much misgiving. Sussex was of all the counties of England the one he loved best, but—it was a fighting area, and the spot I had chosen for my new home, was it, or was it not, within the twenty-mile radius from the coast ? (If it was without it, then only by an inch or two !) In case of invasion, should I not risk another evacuation ? I said that I preferred to be in a fighting area. If I must be *in* a war I would rather be *of* it. He has grown accustomed to his stormy petrel of a sister who, as a child, startled her father by nightly imploring the Almighty in her prayers to " let things happen to me, nice or nasty—and go on happening. I want to feel *everything*," and then, of course, his only wish for me is that I shall be happy. Therefore he strove to hide his apprehensions and listened patiently while I babbled of woods and waters.

The step taken, I became at once happier in mind. My little ' Sunset House ' in Provence would probably be taken from me by Germans or Italians, but now I had once again a corner of my very own and, for five years and perhaps longer, could work out my own salvation and perhaps still be useful.

My landlord recommended me a builder who would effect such alterations to my cottage as I considered vitally necessary, and henceforth I slipped down to Sussex whenever I could to superintend his work, often spending lovely lonely hours planning the arrangement of my little house or perched on a stepping-stone above one of the waterfalls munching an apple or a sausage roll in hot sunshine. One of the gardeners, seeing me there one day, brought me a jugful of heavenly icy water to drink, brought from a hidden spring. Sometimes I would see my White Lady wandering in the woods, a beautiful red setter galloping before her in chase of rabbits, and she would pass by my cottage to see how things were getting on. Once, when I climbed up to the great house to catch my coach outside its gates, I summoned courage to beat a tiny tattoo on the toy door-knocker of the little lodge where she dwelt, but, before I could do it, the door opened and she appeared suddenly before me, her hands held vertically before her, the fingers stretched fanwise, each capped by a small white paper boat. Startling.

" For my babies," she said as she smilingly rocked the little flotilla. " I will take them presently, but first you must come in and have some tea."

Such a tiny little room, but to gain the illusion of height she had painted blue sky and white cumulus clouds on the trap-door in the ceiling opening into a loft. Here in this lodge she lived, while babies from the slums romped in the great rooms of her home and ruined parquet and panelling, riotously happy and free.

"I keep one small room there for my music," she confided to me. I had been told that she was a great artist—a finished violinist who could have been world-famous had she been allowed to be a professional player.

"It is difficult to work at one's music during a war," she sighed. "But perhaps, when you come here and are writing down in the valley, I shall make music again on my mountain."

I found my builder rather Provençal in his methods. We did not progress very quickly with our alterations. He had a habit of disappearing for a week or more with his few remaining men, and I would go down to Sussex only to find a silent locked-up cottage with its key hung on a nail in the dog-kennels behind it (in Provence it would have been left under a saucepan), and I would rage and fume impotently, because there was no telephone down which I could have strafed him. A wasted day, save that I could still take measurements for my curtains, and see if—and where—my stored furniture could be fitted in. After one of these maddening interruptions I received from my builder an explanatory postcard: "I beg Your Ladyship's pardon for the delay in finishing your jobs, but I have been so busy burying people. Two German airmen last week —Government Order."

I had not realised that my builder was also the local undertaker.

I was being pressed by the Transport Manager of the firm from which I had bought my furniture. Every day more of his men were being called up, and delivery became more and more difficult —vans were being taken off, petrol was scarce ; in case of invasion, the roads would be closed, and then it would be impossible to bring down my goods. More than all, he feared that if London were bombed I might lose all my furniture. He longed to get it out of his depository and into my cottage. Henceforth I hustled and pleaded with workmen until, at last, I could write to that Transport Manager and give him a choice of dates for the delivery of my furniture.

" I do not know how you will be able to deliver it," I told him. " I propose to live at the bottom of a precipice with no road to my cottage. The right-of-way through the woods is too narrow for a lorry to pass. I can only suggest delivery by way of mule or parachute. But, if you will fix a day and send me strong, patient, and courageous men who will be kind to me and only laugh at any difficulties or misfortunes that we may have, we may—somehow—be able to achieve the im-possible—IF the weather is fine. I have ordered a barrel of beer to comfort your men when —and if—they reach the foot of my mountain."

Then I took counsel of my new neighbours, who all proved charming, and only too eager to help ' The Lady of the Lake,' as I was

immediately named. Offers to house and to feed
me during these days of transition were gratefully accepted, and suggestions made by those
who knew the lie of the country eagerly adopted.
There was, it appeared, another right-of-way
through the woods on the other side of the
valley, narrow and, in winter, impracticable,
when the grass track became a soggy swamp,
and, if not bogged early on the journey, a car
or cart might slide down the final steep slope
into the lowest of the lakes. But in the month
of August a lorry could easily traverse two
fields and then be unloaded ; my furniture be
stacked on to a farm-cart, and, held in place
by the strong, patient, and courageous men,
the cortége could proceed in comparative safety
down the grass track through the woods, and,
if the cart did not gain an uncontrollable
momentum as it reached the bottom of the
decline, *might* avoid immersion in the lake
immediately below it.

Anyway, this was the only possible method
for transport since *my* right-of-way was far too
narrow, boasted a gradient of 1 in 3, and no
car-tyres or horse's hooves could possibly hold
on slippery rock-face.

Naturally I gratefully accepted the only
alternative and the permission to pass by on
the other side of the lake.

I foresaw an adventurous day ahead of me.

Two days before it, I telephoned to the
Transport Manager to ask him if all was in
order.

"You have warned your men how awful

it's going to be ? " I asked anxiously. " They won't get cross with me ? "

" I am sending a picked team, My Lady," he assured me, " all good fellows. I must admit that Your Ladyship's letter made me long to join in the adventure."

" Oh, I *wish* you'd come," I urged. " If we can only laugh over our inevitable agonies it ought to be great fun." But of course he could not. However, this conversation heartened me greatly and my only anxiety was now about the weather.

Soon after my return to England I had acquired a cockle-shell of a car, at second-hand, to enable me to visit those eight hospitals housing French wounded soldiers. For some time I had tried to do this visiting by the aid of motor-coaches and buses, but the reduced services and difficulty of making cross-country connections proved so tiring, and such a waste of time. By the end of a day I was exhausted, chiefly by standing ; standing about waiting for a bus, sometimes inside a bus, and then beside beds in emergency huts not as yet equipped with chairs. Then one day I saw a squat little grey car, perching like a pigeon on the pavement outside a garage. " MY car," I said to myself and went in and bought it. Not only did the proprietor of the garage decarbonise and revise its engine for me, but he also threw in a completely new battery ; proving that trusting fools, who know nothing of machinery, can safely put themselves into the hands of experts IF they confess their ignorance and throw themselves upon the mercy of the salesman.

I have tested this truism both in France and in England.

My only doubt about my car was whether it could climb my precipice. It was certainly tiny enough to pass down the narrow right-of-way through the woods, and, if my landlord kept his promise to tar and feather the outcrops of surface rock, the tyres would hold the ground. But, could a 7.8 horse-power car ever make that precipitous ascent? I was assured that, in lowest gear, a Baby Austin could climb up the side of a house.

I must admit that my trial trips in this miniature car, round and round and up and down the drive and shrubberies of my brother's Rectory were anxious experiences. I had been used to driving a large, heavy 14-H.P. Fiat saloon which, nevertheless, turned in its own length like a taxi. After the solidarity of my ' Désirée,' this tiny changeling seemed like a soap-bubble, light and wayward, blown about by every breeze (or was it my nervous driving ?), and, when I wanted to turn her, she revolved in an incredibly wide circle to the detriment of various distant shrubs.

I was assured that, once I became accustomed to her little ways, I should never want to drive a big car again, and I am proving this to be true.

The loading up of my cockle-shell, on the day before that fixed for the installation of my furniture in the Sussex cottage, proved to be rather a difficult and arduous business, but at length, with the aid of my four nieces, two girl guests (evacuees), and the 'Nannie,' a quart measure was eventually put into a pint pot, the overflow (unmanageable coats, dressing-gown, and shady hats) streaming over the vacant bucket-seat by my side and cascading above the suitcases piled up on the back seat, until the little car resembled that of an itinerant vendor of old clothes.

At the last moment, the children's dear 'Nannie,' known to us all as 'Babu,' pushed in a cardboard box containing the sum total of my rations of sugar and tea for the weeks that I had lived in the Rectory. As housekeeper, she had hoarded my allowance for the time when I should start housekeeping myself, with no reserve behind me. She also handed me a meat and vegetable meal in a little tin pot for my Blackness, knowing that I should lunch with him *en route*. It is thoughts such as these which make life worth while.

Good-byes are always painful, but in this case it was only 'Au revoir,' for I knew of the glad welcome that I should always receive whenever I could return to those beloved people. Nevertheless, my heart was sad as I left that cluster of dear faces, for, in these days of war, and death falling from the skies, no one can be sure if they will ever meet again, even if they part for an hour. . . .

The Blackness was splendidly well and in tearing spirits from the moment of my arrival. He pushed a cold wet nose into my pocket and filched therefrom my handkerchief, well remembering the chase that would surely ensue. I noticed, happily, that lack of exercise had deprived him of none of his agility. The kennel-man fetched a deck chair for me, placed it in the grass run, and then tactfully departed so that Dominie and I might enjoy a confidential luncheon *à deux;* and I was able to tell him that very soon OUR cottage would be ready for us, and that I had bought him a beautiful Sussex basket of plaited rushes with, also, a green blanket and cushion to match the colour-scheme of the house. Only three months more of this awful separation.

Having been born without a bump of locality, the war-time precaution of blank sign-posts was, to me, peculiarly disheartening. Nor am I much good at map-reading, for always I seem to get wrapped up inside a voluminous map, with difficulty extricate myself, and then spend profane and unsuccessful minutes endeavouring to fold up the intractable thing. My Historian husband had always done the map-reading for me, and all I had ever had to do was to drive serenely on, obeying military orders. This journey was very different, but, as always, I was rescued from every dilemma by some kind policeman or passer-by, amused by my queer assortment of refugee-baggage and arrested by my usual signal of distress, two uplifted hands pressed together in an attitude of prayer. So that at last, having lost myself only the minimum of times, I eventually arrived at the house of hospitable

American friends of my sister's to whom I had once lent my Domaine in Grasse and who I had happily discovered to be my near neighbours in Sussex. Here, I had been invited to stay during the agony of installation in my cottage, and it was lovely to sink into a luxurious bed under a friendly roof after my tiring journey, and to feel sure of help and support from the kindest people in the world during the hectic days that must surely follow.

I was feeling very cockahoop because, a few days before, in London, I had had a stroke of extraordinary good luck. After visiting the quarters of the French Red Cross in London, I had noticed a tall and strikingly good-looking woman descending the steps. She had white hair, wonderful (natural) pink cheeks and clear blue eyes which looked kindly and unflinchingly straight into mine as I asked her the way to Victoria Station. She directed me thither in a voice with a delicious trace of Scots accent.

Then she asked me if by any chance I knew of some work that she might do for the French soldiers in England. Was there a canteen or club that she could, perhaps, supervise ? " I was for many years manageress of the Scotch tea-rooms in Nice," she added modestly. I nearly fell on her neck. How often had I devoured Scotch girdle cakes and drop-scones in that same tea-house !

" I have been trying for a year to get some war work in England," she confided. " I put in for Postal Censorship because I can speak French, but apparently the Government don't want me." She smiled ruefully: "So now I am trying for catering or canteen work, but I can find *no one* who wants me."

"*I* do," I said firmly. "I'm a French refugee and I've taken an abandoned gamekeeper's cottage in a wooded valley at the foot of a precipice. I must go on writing books, so there'll be no time to cook for myself. Will you come and look after me? I'll try to make you happy."

She smiled at my impetuosity. "I can show you my references. I have them here with me," she said.

"I don't want to see them. Your eyes tell me what you are," I told her.

"I'd love to come," she decided quietly.

And so I swept her off to Victoria Station with me, and, over cups of coffee in the tea-room, we discussed details and made our plans. She insisted upon showing me her references, which, of course, were excellent. By an extraordinary coincidence, she was living with her sister in the lovely Sussex village next to mine, and the familiar green coach would deposit her at the gates of my right-of-way. She could thus live with her sister until the cottage was ready and, joy of joys, come daily to help me with its arrangement.

My wonderful Scots lady would be waiting for me and, subsequently, my furniture at the cottage door the next morning. I fell asleep in that super-bed, after my long journey to Sussex, warmed and comforted by this certainty.

CHAPTER XXVIII.

"MANY WATERS."

THE next day dawned. A FINE day, thank heaven. For weeks I had been haunted by those words of my landlord, "in case of bad weather, rain may pour down the right-of-way in torrential floods." In my experience, the weather was generally foul on days of removal and installation of furniture, and I had wondered weakly just what would happen to us all on this occasion if it were. My imagination would only picture the most fantastic things, and so I had resolutely curbed it. But to-day the blessed sun shone down upon a cheerful country-side, and I rose early with a nice tickling sense of amusement and adventure ahead of me.

The first experiment of that day was a trial descent of my right-of-way in the heavily-laden cockle-shell. Beneath the shadow of over-hanging beech trees, planted high above a cliff of rocks, I started my adventure, and I was glad to be making it alone. With relief, I saw that my landlord had been faithful to his promise; the patches of bare rock had been tarred and pebbled, and, lower down where a hidden spring filtered through clay, cinders had been thickly strewn. If I could manœuvre the car round a certain hairpin bend without ditching her, thereafter my passage to the cottage would be fairly easy, for, in this hot August weather, the turf was hard and dry.

Slipping into lowest gear, with foot and hand-brakes in use, I started. The little car rocked like a ship over the uneven surface of rock, but the tyres held it. There was an anxious lurch when I was obliged to climb the bank to get round the hairpin bend, but I narrowly avoided the drainage gully on either side and, with a triumphant shout, safely turned the corner. Chanting a song of victory I continued on my way, now over springy turf fringed with bracken. I inhaled the hot, fusty, ferny smell of it and was at once transported to Windsor Great Park where I used to flounder, shoulder-high, through thickets of it with John. How he would have loved this little secret place that I had found, these noble beech trees and the eternal sound of running water, always associated with his Devon home!

I found my Scots lady, as I knew I should, already cleaning hard inside the cottage, her pink face pinker still from her exertions. But to-day those clear blue eyes wore a troubled look. Was she regretting already the impulsive step she had taken? Then came the shattering truth. Having waited for over a year for an answer to her application for work as a Postal Censor, the Government had accepted her that morning. Important work for the war; good pay; interesting work for which she had always longed. But she had engaged to come to me and felt that she could not let me down. . . .

" But *of course* you must go," I assured her, vehemently, wondering if my bursting heart was showing a bulge in my body as it descended slowly but surely into my feet. I had once watched a snake swallowing a rabbit.

Would the day which had promised so well at dawning continue in this very damping manner ? Probably, now, my lorry-load of furniture would get lost on the road, and the farmer's cart which was to meet it would either fail to appear, or, appearing, would, when loaded with divan-beds, wardrobes, &c., slide gracefully into the lake at the foot of the descent. Well—a lake provided an easy end to these small annoyances. . . .

" What *is* that noise ? " I said, rushing out of the cottage.

Distant yells and shouts of laughter echoed down my rocky valley from the woods behind the cottage. It could only come from the throats of my picked team of strong, patient, and courageous men. Already they were making merry over this adventure. Thank heaven for that. And thank heaven there is something humorous, or oddly ironic, to be found in nearly every situation ; and always heaven to thank for all sorts of lovely things. Also, if life were made too easy for us our muscles would waste and our brains would rot.

Another howl of mirth. I ran to the corner of the lake, where the grass track traversing the woods ended abruptly at the foot of a fairly steep decline, separated only from the water by a narrow path. If things were going to happen to my furniture, this was where they were bound to occur.

Why they did not, I still do not know, for, when I first sighted the cavalcade, the horse was in the act of sitting down, the more easily to slide into the lake, and the s. p. and c. men were very nearly helpless with laughter. They surrounded the over-laden cart, supporting divans and toppling wardrobes and tables lest they shoot over the head of the subsiding horse into the water.

I hoped that if they did, they would float, and wondered if the remainder of our day would be spent in aquatic sports.

Happily, the horse was hauled to its feet before it finally sat down, and, after a hectic few moments of frantic effort, the furniture was balanced once more, the cart lurched to the left and was safely upon the path encircling the lowest lake, about three hundred yards from the cottage. From thence its progress was more dignified, for the ground was flat, and when we reached the rough grass surrounding the cottage the men thought it better to transport the heavier objects on their broad backs.

At the front door they were received by my Stolen Jewel, very upright and expectant, ready to cope, with Scots thoroughness, with any situation. She continued to cope throughout the day, marshalling her men like a General of the A.S.C. while my builder plied them with beer, and as I watched her quiet efficiency and method I gnashed my spiritual teeth.

Well—thanks to *Mademoiselle's* training in camp and in our tiny escape-places, the dolls' cottage on the rocks outside St Tropez, and our converted *bergerie* in the High Alps — I had learned to be orderly in the kitchen and less tremulous with cooking utensils. I could always cook for myself in my cottage, using all those lovely green saucepans and green-handled gadgets ; and, for my company, in three months' time I should have Dominie, and I should also have foxes, badgers, hedgehogs, rabbits, every kind of tree-bird and water-fowl ; but I hoped NOT " snakes of unnatural dimensions." There is nothing cosy or companionable about a snake. Solitude holds no terrors for me, because I know that I am never alone—but I wondered, a little wistfully, when I should have time to write, and, if I ever found time, whether I should be too weary to think.

I realised that I was subconsciously trying to hearten my own discouragement (caused by the very first reverse of fortune that I had so far suffered in England), and that I was standing on the edge of the abyss of Self-Pity into which so many weaklings. fall. This was probably caused by emptiness inside, for mental depression is generally caused by physical condition. Well, the remedy was simple. We would call a halt and eat.

The men were delighted to knock off work for an hour, and they wandered off into the shade of the woods carrying their picnic packages with them. The wonderful Scots lady produced a loaf, a pat of butter, and some slices of ham that she had bought in her village before catching the coach, knowing that we should have no time or inclination to open some of my ' hard stores ' sent down with the furniture.

We carried our food to the edge of the lake so that we might enjoy it in full sunshine while gloating over the view which seemed to become lovelier every moment. My companion told me that her services were mine for the next two days. She could at anyrate help me to clean cupboards, paper shelves, and to unpack, wash and place crockery before she took up her Government work the following week.

Already the wind was being tempered for the shorn lamb.

The rest of the day passed off merrily enough, the men had all fallen under the spell of this enchanted place, and, mellowed by sunshine and beer, were envying me the life I should lead as the 'Lady of the Lake.'

They left me at last, wishing me happiness in my new home, saying how much they had enjoyed their "outing in the country," and the farm-cart, this time laden with a laughing human freight, conveyed them back through the woods to their waiting motor-van. My Scots lady then took her leave. The dreaded day had passed without misadventure.

Alone, I stayed awhile, dreaming. The sun was sinking now and its lengthening beams shone through the trees and lit the lakes with an almost unearthly radiance. It was the magic moment of the red ray, when every flower becomes a jewel and every leaf translucent. God walking in his garden.

A snoring intermittent drone above my head reminded me that we were at war. The Huns were paying us their evening visit.

I prayed heaven that they should never be allowed to spoil my lovely valley; and that no flaming sword should bar me from this Paradise that I had found. . . .

.   .   .   .

March 1941.

I am sitting in my little green room. It is very cosy with a log-fire crackling and lamplight falling softly upon a bowl of wild daffodils picked in the woods yesterday. Spring is nearly here—and Dominie, quite. At intervals my elbow is jogged by a wet black indiarubber nose to remind me of this. Not that I need reminding, for, ever since he returned from his rabbit-riot in the woods, he has been worrying the towel with which I dry his feathered feet, blitzing around mine while German aeroplanes blitz over my head.

Somewhere, a bomb. One less for poor old London, anyway. . . . My Blackness hears the far-off barrage guns, rolls an apprehensive eye at me, but does not tremble. That sound became familiar to him while he was in the quarantine kennels, but he knows that it is evil. I was always in great fear that a bomb might shatter the confining barriers and little dogs make terrified escape, to be for ever lost. But now we are together again, Dominie and I, to share as bravely as two gun-shy people can, whatever is to come, as we shared the danger and anguish of France.

France! When I hear that name it is as though a great hand squeezed my heart. But, whereas for many months the thought of France held only horror and hopelessness, now I see a star of hope shining above her lovely mountains.

General de Gaulle is rallying the loyal Frenchmen of North Africa; the French people are waking from the anæsthesia of defeat and despair; they have ceased to believe England hostile; but, disarmed; spied upon, day and night, by the Gestapo; their bodies starved by Germany and their minds fed only with lies by traitorous Vichy politicians, who have sold themselves to the devil; at present they are powerless to help us—or themselves. But we know now that the truth filters through that cloud of poison gas and that they rejoice in our victories and grow restive under the German yoke. Cable communication is established between England and Unoccupied France and I can talk once more with *Mademoiselle*. To-day came a cable from her saying that her heart is with us all in England, but that the nights

and days are long. She and little Squibs are
alone now in the *Château*, but I am sure that
she is growing food for the hungry peasants and
that Squibs is keeping down the rats.

To make her life easier in her isolation,
Mademoiselle has been persuaded to regain her
American nationality.

How proud she must be to-night of her
America, for early this morning the B.B.C.
relayed parts of President Roosevelt's speech,
made after the passing of the Lease-and-Lend
Bill. Dominie and I listened with eyes on
stalks as we heard that strong voice promising
swift and staggering aid to England. His soul-
stirring message of help and hope is ringing
still in my heart as it must ring in the hearts
of every inhabitant of this little, little island.
It is so wonderful to know that tiny Mother
England, with her lovely war-scarred face and
indomitable heart, has so lusty and loyal a
daughter, overseas, to love and support her
in her hour of need.

To-night ' The Lady of the Lake ' would like
to snatch some of those brilliant silver stars
from the sky wherewith to spangle her hair ;
to tear from the firmament those ice-stripes,
made by the hot propellers of German bombers,
to wave as banners heralding the sure and
certain victory of freed democracies.

Printed in Great Britain by
WILLIAM BLACKWOOD & SONS LTD.

PERFUME FROM PROVENCE
Lady Fortescue

In the early 1930s, Winifred Fortescue and her husband, Sir John Fortescue, left England and settled in Provence, in a small stone house amid olive groves, on the border of Grasse. Their exodus had been caused partly by ill health, but mostly for financial reasons, for it was in the period between the wars when it was cheaper to live in France than in England.

Almost at once they were bewitched, by the scenery, by their garden – an incredible terraced landscape of vines, wild flowers, roses and lavender – and above all by the charming, infuriating, warm-hearted and wily Provençals. The house – called the Domaine – was delightful but tiny, and at once plans were put in hand to extend it over the mountain terraces. Winifred Fortescue's witty and warm account of life with stone masons, builders, craftsmen, gardeners, and above all her total involvement with the everyday events of a Provençal village, made *Perfume From Provence* an instant bestseller that went into several editions and became a famous and compulsive book for everyone who has ever loved France, most especially Provence.

0 552 99479 0

BLACK SWAN

THE BOTTLEBRUSH TREE
A Village in Andalusia
Hugh Seymour-Davies

'IT IS PURE JOY'
The Tablet

When Hugh Seymour-Davies and his wife decided to buy a house in Spain they had a very definite dream of what it should be – old, graceful, inexpensive, a sunny open house far from human habitation in countryside of great beauty. What they found was a small near-windowless home, built on many steep levels, in the heart of an Andalusian mountain village. Here, the first strangers to settle in the community, they were warmly accepted by their neighbours who pushed jovially into their lives at all times with a complete disregard for privacy (Rosalia, the custodian of their house key during absences, even insisting on one occasion on conducting a long conversation with her patron through the lavatory door).

In the village the year revolved around the *ferias* of Easter, San Anton, and Candelaria, and around the gruelling tending of crops which were the lifeblood of the peasant farmers – the grapes and almonds and olives, culminating in the sweated labour of raisin-making and almond-husking, of wine-making (the aromatic, rich, druggy, honey-coloured wine of the area) and olive-picking.

Andalusia, its scenery, its customs and its people are beautifully evoked in this enchanting and humorous account of life in an ancient and alien land.

'AN ATTRACTIVE, MAINLY LIGHT-HEARTED ACCOUNT OF ANGLO-SAXON RESPONSES TO A CULTURE VERY DIFFERENT FROM OURS, OF A LIKING FOR THE PRIMITIVE, AND A RELUCTANCE TO SEE IT VANISH'
Catholic Herald

'PERCEPTIVE AND EXUBERANTLY ENTERTAINING'
Lookout

0 552 99658 0

BLACK SWAN

JOGGING ROUND MAJORCA
Gordon West

Has all the nostalgic appeal of the bestselling *Perfume From Provence*.

In the 1920s, Gordon West and his wife decided they wanted to go somewhere unexplored and unspoiled, right off the beaten tourist route. They settled on the little-known island of Majorca.

Travelling via Paris and Barcelona, they finally boarded the small white steamboat which was to take them to the idyllic Bay of Palma, and there they began their exploration of the enchanting island, sometimes in hair-raising motor rides round steep cliffs and on unmade roads, sometimes by mule, and more often on foot. They lodged in simple hotels, small houses, and once in a monastery, and everywhere they observed the rich pageantry of a people whose customs, gentle manners, and generous hospitality made Majorca a unique and fascinating place.

As read on Radio 4 by Leonard Pearcey.

0 552 99601 7

BLACK SWAN

BY BUS TO THE SAHARA
Gordon West

It was in the 1930s that Gordon and Mary West decided to
explore the land of palm groves and oases, mosques and
muezzins, and the ancient walled cities of an old Empire – by
bus. Setting off from Tilbury with two suitcases, a large
painting box, and a roll of artist's canvas, they sailed to
Tangier, and there entered the world of French Morocco, a
world of sheiks and harems, the ancient Berber tribes of the
Atlas Mountains, of French Legionnaires drinking
'earthquakes' in seedy desert bars, of beautiful old Moorish
palaces and mountain mud villages.

Once they had trained across the hazardous territory of
Spanish Morocco, still in the throes of fighting the Spanish
Civil War, they began their real journey on native buses,
racketing hundreds of miles across Morocco and packed in
with Arabs, soldiers, sheep, chickens and every variety of
baggage. Their route took them to the great romantic cities of
the desert world – Rabat, Marrakech, Meknes – and also to
tiny oases villages that no one had ever heard of. They met
and were befriended by fire-eaters, sorcerers, slave dealers,
holy men, and descendants of The Prophet.

By Bus to the Sahara captures perfectly the colourful, exotic
and little-explored country of Morocco and the desert in a
vanished era.

0 552 99666 1

BLACK SWAN

THE HOUSE BY THE DVINA
A RUSSIAN CHILDHOOD
by Eugenie Fraser

A unique and moving account of life in Russia before, during and immediately after the Revolution, *The House by the Dvina* is the fascinating story of two families, separated in culture and geography, but bound together by a Russian-Scottish marriage. It includes episodes as romantic and dramatic as any in fiction: the purchase by the author's great-grandfather of a peasant girl with whom he had fallen in love; the desperate journey by sledge in the depths of winter made by her grandmother to intercede with Tsar Aleksandr II for her hushand; the extraordinary courtship of her parents; and her Scottish granny being caught up in the abortive revolution of 1905.

Eugenie Fraser herself was brought up in Russia but was taken on visits to Scotland. She marvellously evokes the reactions of a child to two totally different environments, sets of customs and family backgrounds. The characters on both sides are beautifully drawn and splendidly memorable.

With the events of 1914 to 1920 – the war with Germany, the Revolution, the murder of the Tsar, the withdrawal of the Allied Intervention in the north – came the disintegration of the country and of family life. The stark realities of hunger, deprivation and fear are sharply contrasted with the day-to-day experiences, joys, frustrations and adventures of childhood. The reader shares the family's suspense and concern about the fates of its members and relives with Eugenie her final escape to Scotland.

'Eugenie Fraser has a wondrous tale to tell and she tells it very well. There is no other autobiography quite like it'
Molly Tibbs, *Contemporary Review*

'A wholly delightful account'
Elizabeth Sutherland, *Scots Magazine*

0 552 12833 3

—— **BLACK SWAN** ——

A SELECTED LIST OF FINE WRITING AVAILABLE FROM CORGI AND BLACK SWAN

99065 5	THE PAST IS MYSELF	*Christabel Bielenberg*	£6.99
99469 3	THE ROAD AHEAD	*Christabel Bielenberg*	£5.99
99600 9	NOTES FROM A SMALL ISLAND	*Bill Bryson*	£6.99
99572 X	STRANGE ANGELS	*Andy Bull*	£5.99
99690 4	TOUCH THE DRAGON	*Karen Connelly*	£6.99
99707 2	ONE ROOM IN A CASTLE	*Karen Connelly*	£6.99
99482 0	MILLENNIUM	*Felipe Fernandez-Armesto*	£14.99
99530 4	HG: THE HISTORY OF MR WELLS	*Michael Foot*	£7.99
99479 0	PERFUME FROM PROVENCE	*Lady Fortescue*	£6.99
12833 3	THE HOUSE BY THE DVINA	*Eugenie Fraser*	£6.99
14539 4	THE DVINA REMAINS	*Eugenie Fraser*	£6.99
12555 5	IN SEARCH OF SCHRÖDINGER'S CAT	*John Gribbin*	£7.99
99637 8	MISS McKIRDY'S DAUGHTERS WILL NOW DANCE THE HIGHLAND FLING	*Barbara Kinghorn*	£6.99
14433 9	INVISIBLE CRYING TREE	*Christopher Morgan & Tom Shannon*	£6.99
99504 5	LILA	*Robert Pirsig*	£6.99
14322 7	THE MAZE	*Lucy Rees*	£6.99
99579 7	THE HOUSE OF BLUE LIGHTS	*Joe Roberts*	£6.99
99658 0	THE BOTTLEBRUSH TREE	*Hugh Seymour-Davies*	£6.99
99638 6	BETTER THAN SEX	*Hunter S. Thompson*	£6.99
99601 7	JOGGING ROUND MAJORCA	*Gordon West*	£5.99
99666 1	BY BUS TO THE SAHARA	*Gordon West*	£6.99
99366 2	THE ELECTRIC KOOL AID ACID TEST	*Tom Wolfe*	£7.99

All Transworld titles are available by post from:

Book Service By Post, PO Box 29, Douglas, Isle of Man, IM99 1BQ

Credit cards accepted. Please telephone 01624 675137, fax 01624 670923 or Internet http://www.bookpost.co.uk or e-mail: bookshop@enterprise.net for details.

Free postage and packing in the UK. Overseas customers: allow £1 per book (paperbacks) and £3 per book (hardbacks).